Sincerely, Carter

Sincerely, Carter

WHITNEY GRACIA WILLIAMS

Cover design by Najla Qambers of Najla Qambers Designs
Editing by Evelyn Guy of Indie Edit Guy

ISBN: 1512303631
ISBN 13: 9781512303636

For Tamisha Draper.

You are literally the BEST BFF a girl could ever ask for...

Thank you for the endless Starbucks meet-ups and conversations that led to the creation of this book!

(And yes...I'm gratefully aware that the 'Sincerely, Carter' title was your idea...)

(And no, Chris Draper, I will not credit you just because you're her husband...LOL)

prologue

Carter

I can still remember, with the type of clarity that makes the hairs on the back of my neck stand up, the very beginning of bullshit. At least, in my own life.

I was ten years old, and my parents—"The James' at 1100 Joyce Avenue," were holding a fundraiser in our home. In the middle of the thousand-dollar-a-plate dinner, my father decided to give an unnecessary speech.

There he was—six foot four, genuine American blue eyes, and genuinely greedy, talking about how he wanted to invest in healthier menus for the kids in school. He also wanted to help invest in better disciplinary ideals since he knew of a certain child (it was me) who couldn't stay out of trouble to save his life.

Still, none of those ideals warranted the bullshit label—the next ones did: As he was toasting to all of his sponsors in the room, he lifted his glass and said, "I consider everyone here tonight to be a friend of mine. If you're not a friend, it's only because you're family, and family is forever. The main reason I'm saying this right now is because my own late father taught me a very important lesson that has stuck with me for all these years: Some people come into your life for a reason, some a season, and some a lifetime."

There was loud applause, lots of cheering and heartfelt "So true...So true..." responses tossed around the room at that moment. And then an older man stooped down to my level and said, "Your father is right, you know? Remember everything he just said."

"What did he just say?"

"He said some people come into your life for a reason, some a season, and some a lifetime." He smiled. "You should keep that in mind as much as you can in your life." He winked at me and walked away.

I didn't know it then, but my father and his fickle follower had practically predicted my future...

A few years after he gave that speech, he must've figured he'd obliged his "reason" in me and my mom's life because he left us both. Several years after that, my mother decided her "season" of motherhood was done, and decided that she was tired of being a mom—that her real calling could be found in smoke bars and casinos. As far as for 'a lifetime,' I could only think of one person who ever came close...

fourth grade

Carter

Dear Miss Carpenter,

I am sorry that I was bad in class yesterday. I did not mean to cause a dissrupshun, and I am sorry that I broke your best pens, but I am not sorry that I HATE Arizona Turner.

She is ugly and she talks way too much. I don't know why you never send her to the office like you send me. She deserves to be punish too, and I hope she dies tomorrow so I won't have to see her or her ugly metal mouth anymore.

Sincerely,
Carter

I smiled and handed the letter to my mom, hoping that this time would be the charm—that she wouldn't make me rewrite it all over again.

I was beyond tired of Arizona getting me into trouble and laughing about it. She thought she was so smart because she knew the answers to all the questions in class, but I knew them, too. Especially because I knew where our teacher kept the answer key and I always stole it at lunchtime.

My parents knew her parents personally because they always had to go to conferences about me "picking on her" and "making her cry," but no one believed me when I told them that she was the one who started it.

She always started it…

"Carter…" My mom took a deep breath and shook her head. "This is a terrible letter. It's worse than the last three you wrote."

"How? I didn't call Arizona any names this time. I just said I wanted her to die."

"You don't think you're hurting her feelings whenever you call her ugly?"

"She is ugly."

"She's not ugly." My father stepped into the room. "Now, those braces in her mouth might be, but as a whole? She's pretty cute."

"Seriously?" My mom glared at him, and he laughed.

"Sorry." He walked over and patted me on the back. "It's not nice to call someone ugly, son. No matter how much you hate her. You've got to stop letting this Arizona girl get to you. This is the fifth time this year you've gotten in trouble."

"Eighth time." My mother corrected him. "He pushed her off the swings when she was in mid-air last week."

My father looked at me. "And what did you do this time?"

I didn't answer him. I looked down at the floor instead.

"He stood up in the middle of a math test and said, 'I hate you, Arizona,'" my mom said. "He then proceeded to grab the poor girl's test paper, ball it up, and throw it across the room… He missed and knocked his teacher's favorite glass pens to the floor."

Shaking his head, my dad sighed. "Just stop talking to this girl, okay? Don't even look her way. You're going to have to learn to ignore her, no matter what. Something tells me she won't be a 'lifetime' person for you anyway. She's just seasonal, so she'll go away soon. Trust me."

"Glad to see you finally acting like an adult about this." My mom ripped my letter in half and focused her attention on me.

"Now, sit down and write a nice letter to your teacher, an even nicer one to Arizona, and tell her that you're not going to be mean to her anymore. Try to think of something nice to say, too. Maybe mention something about those pretty dresses she always wears?"

I groaned, but I picked up my pen and wrote.

It took me five more letters to get it right since she made me take out the words "stupid," "hate," and "die," but I finally got it perfect around midnight. Then I promised myself that after I gave Arizona my letter tomorrow, I would never ever speak to her again...

———

The next day at school, I set the sorry note on my teacher's desk super early and walked down the farthest row—plopping down in the very last seat. Then I took out my homework and tried to finish a few more math questions before class started.

I counted four times seven on my fingers and saw Arizona taking the seat next to me.

"Good morning, Carter," she said.

I pretended that I didn't hear her.

"Carter?" She tapped my shoulder and I wrote twenty eight on my paper.

"Hello?" She tapped my shoulder even harder. "Carter? *Carter*?"

"*WHAT*?!" I finally looked at her.

"Don't you have something for me today? Something nice and important?" She smiled her huge mouth of metal.

Ugh. She's so ugly... "Nope."

"Your mom didn't make you write me another 'I'm very sorry' note?" She crossed her arms. "Because that's exactly what she told my mom on the phone this morning."

"Well, your mom must be deaf and dumb because I didn't write anything for *you*."

"*What?*" She gasped. "Take that back or I'll snitch!"

"Go ahead and snitch!" I shrugged, waiting for her to raise her hand and tell on me like always.

She didn't. She just stared at me. Then she reached into her pocket and tossed a folded note onto my desk.

I wanted to crumple it into a ball and throw it right at her face like I should have done yesterday, but I opened it instead and read:

Dear Carter,

I am sorry that I made you act bad and break Miss Carpenter's pens yesterday, but I am not sorry that I HATE you. You are ugly and you talk way too much. That's why I always get you in trouble because you can't shut up and you think you know everything BUT YOU DON'T! I really wish you will get hit by a bus one day soon because you suck. You suck A LOT.

Not Sincerely,

Arizona

We became best friends that very day...

track 1. blank space (3:47)

Carter

Present Day

The sex just isn't enough anymore…

I shook my head as my current girlfriend, Emily, ran in circles around me on the beach. Dressed in a bright red bikini, she smiled as she splashed me, garnering the jealous attention of other guys nearby. Every so often, when I smiled back at her, she would untie the camera from her wrist and stand next to me—holding it high above us while yelling, "Selfie time! Cutest Couple Everrr!"

To be honest, everything about this woman was damn near perfect on the outside: She was stunningly beautiful with light green eyes and full soft lips; she had an infectious laugh that could make the most sullen person smile, and her sense of humor was pretty similar to mine. She had a naturally bubbly personality that could make any stranger believe she was a best friend at a first encounter, and behind closed doors, her desire for sex was almost as high as mine.

That's where her nice qualities ended though, and I unfortunately found that out much too late.

A few months after we started to date seriously, her true character began to show: First, I found out that her naturally bubbly personality wasn't "natural" at all; it was a side effect of the illegal Adderall she often abused and overdosed. Second, was her habit of texting me every hour on the hour with "I miss you, baby. Where are you?" whenever we weren't together. If I didn't answer her in three minutes or less, she would text me repeatedly: "Are you dead? ARE. YOU. DEAD?!" And lastly, the reason I was definitely ending this relationship sooner than later, was her new and weird-ass sex fetish: She liked to crawl around the room on all fours and purr like a kitten before and after sex. She even "meowed" when she came.

Some shit I just couldn't handle for the long term…

"Hey, you!" Emily splashed me, knocking me out of my thoughts. "What are you over there thinking about?"

"A lot of things…" I admitted.

"That's why I like you, Carter." She smiled. "You're always in deep thought, thinking about deep things…" She held the camera above us. "Deep-thought selfie!"

"Right…" I waited until she'd snapped the photo. "Are you ready to head back yet?"

"Almost! Give me five minutes. I want to wade farther out and feel the waves against my chest one last time."

I nodded and watched her slip into the ocean—beckoning me to join her, but I simply forced a smile and stayed back. I was still thinking, still wondering why I could never get past the six month mark with any woman I dated—why I could never find enough strength to stick around another second.

"Okay!" Emily met me on the shore. "I'm ready to head back now if you are, Carter. I know what's really on your mind…" She pressed her hand against my crotch. "Meow…"

Jesus…

I moved her hand away and clasped it, leading her back toward my place.

"What do you think about going to the Everglades tomorrow?" she asked.

"I think we should talk about that tomorrow   We actually have a lot to talk about."

"Awww." She squeezed my hand. "It sounds like you're finally going to let me inside and tell me all your deep, dark secrets..."

"I don't have any deep, dark secrets."

"Well, whatever you want to talk about tomorrow, can we *not* talk about it at Gayle's?"

"What?" I looked over at her and raised my eyebrow. "Why not?"

"Because, although I know you love the food there and I do, too, I hate that place. Like, being there, you know?"

"Not really..."

"I just feel like it's not our own 'couple spot', you know? Every couple needs their own "OMG this is our spot" type of place. Speaking of which, I was thinking we need to post more pictures of us together on Facebook. I'll be posting what we took today on tomorrow. What do you think of the caption: "OMG my boyfriend took me on a surprise trip to the beach? Hashtag, he loves me, hashtag, don't be jealous, hashtag, he always spends money on me."

"The beach is free..."

She ignored my comment and continued babbling, eventually transitioning from our social media profiles to how badly she wanted to ride me tonight, but the second we got back to my place, she collapsed onto my bed and fell asleep.

Relieved, I took a beer from the fridge and leaned against the counter. I needed to think tomorrow's break-up through. I needed it to be short, swift, and to the point.

"It's not you, it's me..." "I'm just not sure if I'm really the man you're looking for..." "Okay, look. It's that weird-ass cat shit you do "No, no...I need to be diplomatic about this... Hmmm...

I googled, "Top Ten Best Ways to Break Up with Someone," but the browser crashed and a phone call came through instead. My best friend, Arizona.

"Hello?" I answered.

"Meowwww…." she whispered. "Meowww…Meow!"

"Fuck you, Ari."

She laughed. "Are you busy right now? Am I interrupting something?"

"Not at all." I stepped into my room and tapped the wall to see if Emily would wake up. "I just got back from the beach. Emily passed out as soon as we got back."

"Did she eat too much catnip? That happens to me all the time."

"Is there a point to this goddamn phone call, Ari?"

"There is." She laughed. "There is."

"Care to share it before I hang up on you?"

"Yeah…I think I finally want to have sex with Scott tonight."

"Okay. Then go finally have sex with Scott tonight."

"No, no, no…" Her tone was more serious now. "I'm just not sure if I should or not, you know? I'm getting some vibes…"

"What kind of vibes?"

"That it's not a good idea, that it's not the right time."

I sighed. Arizona always needed to host an internal examination session whenever she was considering sleeping with a guy. Everything had to be measured in terms of risks and returns, down to "the intensity of the kisses," "the average length and quality of the dates," and "the long-term relationship factor." Even though she denied it, I knew she kept a spreadsheet on her phone to track all of those ridiculous factors, and that she started a new one each time she dated someone.

"Look," I said, "if you don't want to sleep with him, don't. Tell him you're not ready yet."

"Do you think he'll be okay with that, though? We've been together eight months."

"What?" I nearly choked on my beer. "It's been *eight months*?"

"See? That's the thing, and I know he feels like tonight is the night since I kind of alluded to it, but…I don't know. I'm not sure if he's worth the risk. I don't want to get burned again…"

"Wait a minute." I shook my head. "Where are you right now?"

"In Scott's apartment."

"Then where the hell is *he*?"

"He went to CVS to get us some condoms."

"At least his heart is in the right place…" I rolled my eyes. "Seriously though, if you're not one hundred percent sure, just tell him what you just told me. He'll have to understand."

"And if he doesn't?"

"Find someone who does."

"Right," she said. "Are you still thinking about breaking up with Emily this weekend, or are you going to try and make it work?"

"No." I walked over to my bedroom door and shut it before completely answering. "It's definitely over. I'm not feeling it anymore, and I'm beyond tired of all the arguing, her erratic craziness, and feeling like I have to check in every hour on the hour."

"This is your fourth breakup in a year. I think it's time for you to give the girlfriend thing a rest."

"Don't worry," I said. "I've finally accepted that I'm not the relationship type, and I'll be making my single status very clear after tomorrow. I need to be single and enjoy life before law school starts anyway."

"So, you're saying that you're going to be a whore this summer?"

"I'm *implying* that." I smiled. "There's a difference."

"There's really not…Oh! Gotta go! Scott just pulled up in the driveway so I'll call you tomorrow. Bye!"

I hung up and grabbed another beer from the fridge. As I was shutting the door, a plate whizzed by my head—inches away from my ear. It hit the wall and shattered onto the floor.

"*What the—*" I turned around to see a red faced Emily. "What the fuck is wrong with you?"

"With me?" She tossed another plate at my head and missed. "What's wrong with *me*? What the fuck is wrong with *you*?!"

"Only one of us is currently using plates as a potential murder weapon right now..."

"You're breaking up with me tomorrow? Days before graduation?"

"If I say yes, will you stop throwing my goddamn plates?"

She threw another one, but it landed near the stove. "I thought we were going on vacation together this summer! I had tons of selfies and sex planned, but all of a sudden you're willing to throw it away? Just like that?" She was talking faster than ever. "I know I text you all the time, but only because I worry and like you so much, and I'm a journalism major so I see stories that would make your mind explode   People are out there dying every day, Carter. Every. Day."

"Okay..." I shook my head. "Exactly *how much* Adderall did you take today?"

"Our perfect future aside, you're breaking up with me and I have to hear about it from a *phone conversation* you're having with someone else? That's messed up, Carter! Beyond messed up!"

"You're right." I held up my hands in a slight surrender. "And I'm actually very sorry about that, but yes, I am breaking up with you tomorrow. Well, right now, actually..." I decided to give diplomatic option one a go. "It's not you, it's me..."

"Are you being serious right now?"

I went for diplomatic option two. "I just don't think I'm the man you're looking for."

She was silent for a long time, glaring at me in utter disbelief. I was hoping she wouldn't try to talk me out of this, otherwise, I'd have to go with the less than diplomatic reason and dodge more plates.

"You know what?" She set down the remaining plates in her hand and slid her bag over her shoulder. Then she walked toward me. "I should've seen this coming miles away; should've known that you would never bare your soul to me like I bared mine to you."

"You're more than welcome to stay the night," I said, glad she was somewhat accepting. "I never said I was putting you out. I can take you home tomorrow."

"Oh! So, now you want to be a gentleman?!" She hissed. "Please! My best friend is outside waiting for me."

"Well, in that case...I'm sorry we didn't work out."

"You're really not," she said, stepping closer. "You're not sorry because you don't really *want* a girlfriend, Carter. You've never wanted one, and do you want to know why?" A slight purr escaped her lips and I was more than convinced that ending this relationship was for the best.

"Ask me why." She pushed my shoulder. "Ask me why you don't need a goddamn girlfriend!"

"Why don't I need a girlfriend, Emily...?"

"Because you already have one...You always have..." She pushed me harder. "And her name *is Arizona Turner*."

I raised my eyebrow, completely confused.

"So, fuck you *and* her, and I hope your tiny little cock—"

"It was *huge* when you were riding it yesterday..."

"Whatever! Fuck. You. Carter." She bumped me with her shoulder and headed toward the side door. She twisted and turned the lock a few times, pushing and pulling on the knob.

"You have to leave through the front door," I said, without moving. "New locks, remember?"

"Oh, yeah...I totally forgot about that. Did I ever tell you that I liked the new locks you picked?" She moved to the front door and opened it, looking over her shoulder. "I liked them a lot, very artsy and unique. How much did you pay for them again?"

I gave her a blank stare.

"Well then…" she said, snapping back into pissed off mode." Goodbye, Carter James…And FUCK YOU AGAIN…With something rough and sand-papery!"

The inevitable door slam came right after.

I walked into my room to see if she'd damaged anything, to see if she'd tried to leave a revenge mark somewhere, and she had. Pictures that were once hanging on my wall—the only ones I had of my parents, were lying all over the floor. She'd even somehow managed to open all my desk drawers and throw everything out without making too much noise.

Why do I continue to do this to myself?

Annoyed, yet relieved that I'd be spending tonight alone, I returned everything to its rightful place—hanging the pictures back up first.

When I finished tossing all of the pencils and pens back into the drawer, I heard my phone ringing in my pocket. Arizona, again.

"Yes?" I held it up to my ear. "Do I need to explain how sex works to you? I know it's been awhile in your world, but it really isn't that difficult…"

"Scott dumped me!"

"What?"

"HE. DUMPED. ME!" She huffed. "But you know what? I'll call and tell you about it tomorrow after I calm down. I don't want Emily accusing you of having phone sex with me."

"Emily actually just left." I searched for my car keys. "We can talk."

"Oh my god, let me tell you then!" Her coherent speech ended right there. Whenever she was discussing a breakup, there was an endless tirade of cursing and "What a goddamn asshole," "He didn't deserve me!" "He's going to miss me!" woes before she ever started to sound intelligible.

"Ari..." I said after she called him a dickhead for the umpteenth time. "Just tell me what happened."

"Right..." She took a deep breath. "He came back with the condoms, and we were suddenly half naked, kissing, and we were close to going there—*so* close...But, those weird vibes came back, so I told him to stop and that I wasn't ready. I said I needed a little more time to make sure I was doing the right thing. Then I said, 'Besides, Carter thinks that I should—"

"Whoa, whoa, whoa..." I stopped, finally locating my car keys. "You brought *me* up?"

"Yeah, why wouldn't I? I told him what you said about me being one hundred percent sure before I slept with someone. Then he said, 'Okay, that's it. We're over. Get the hell out.'"

"He did not tell you to get the hell out, Ari. You're exaggerating."

"He did!" She sounded livid all over again. "As a matter of fact, when I was walking out, he said that since I always have to go ask for your advice about everything, that I should just go and fuck *you.*"

Silence.

At the same time, we both burst into hysterical laughter.

"No offense," I said, still laughing. "But I would *never* fuck you, let alone put up with you in a relationship."

"You mean, *I* would never put up with you. Not only are you the worst boyfriend in the history of boyfriends, you're also not my type."

"Clearly." I opened the 'track-current-caller' app on my phone. "Exceptionally sexy, muscular in all the right places, and the ability to make any woman want to sleep with me after a first date are somehow all unfortunate qualities in your mind."

"Seriously? Are you listening to yourself right now?" She scoffed. "Please. For the record, my qualities are far better and weed out the one-track minded men like yourself: Smart, witty, and talented with something other than my tongue."

"You left out your best quality."

"Which one?"

"The permanent 'not interested in fucking' label etched onto your forehead."

She laughed, and I heard a light knock at the door.

"Hold on a second." I held the phone to my chest and walked to the front door, hoping it wasn't Emily.

It wasn't.

It was Ari, puffy red eyes and all.

"Can I spend the night on your couch since Emily left?" she asked, stepping inside. "It doesn't make sense for me to go all the way back home at this hour, and I'm sort of offended that you didn't at least offer me a ride since I clearly said Scott kicked me out. You know his apartment isn't that far from here."

"I was actually getting ready to come get you." I ended our call.

"Sure you were." Her eyes veered to my arm. "You got *another* tattoo?" She touched my sleeve, tracing the latest addition—another branch of Latin phrases on my overgrown cypress tree. "When was this?"

"Last week. I told you I was considering it."

"Considering, not actually *getting...*" She traced it again. "I like it. Although, you're definitely going to have to wear suits for most of your professional life. No one wants to hire a lawyer with a sleeve full of tattoos."

"So you say." I grabbed a blanket from the hallway closet and handed it to her. "You can take my room. I'll sleep out here. I need to think."

"About how to break up with Emily?"

"No, that's already done. She overheard our conversation and dumped me right before you called."

"Wow. What a suck-fest day for the both of us...." She frowned, but then she quickly snapped back into her usual upbeat self. "You want to grab a late breakfast this Saturday at Gayle's?"

"Sure. Noon?"

"Actually, could we do one o'clock?" She started walking to my room. "I have a bikini wax appointment at noon."

"Why are you waxing the one part of your body that no one ever sees?"

"*I* see it."

"Hmmm. So, is that the real reason you wanted to postpone sleeping with Scott tonight? Because you had a bush you didn't want him to see?"

"*What?* What did you say?"

"I know you, Ari." I smirked. "And you definitely heard me... Is that the real reason?"

"Carter..."

"I've known you since what? Fifth grade?"

"Fourth grade."

"Same thing," I said, noticing a slight redness on her cheeks. "You can tell me. I'm not going to judge you. I'll just suggest you keep your bush trimmed regularly instead of worrying about waxing it all off at the last minute."

"Even if I had a bush," she said, rolling her eyes, "which I *don't*, I'm pretty sure I wouldn't make that the main reasoning behind not having sex with someone—my boyfriend especially, at the last minute."

"Good," I said. "Because most guys—guys like me, honestly don't care about that. And seeing as though you probably won't be having sex for another eight months, I'm just trying to save you some money. Maybe take the money you'll be spending on a wax this weekend and buy a better vibrator instead?"

She slammed the door to my room, and I laughed until I fell asleep.

track 2. wildest dreams. (3:54)

Arizona

Why don't they tell you that the major you declare your sophomore year may be the one subject you end up loathing by your senior year? And how can people honestly expect a nineteen year old to know what she wants to do for the rest of her life and be happy with her decision?

Ridiculous...

Somewhere between Small Business Accounting and Tax Law 101 my junior year, I realized that I hated business only slightly less than I hated the idea of working in an office for the rest of my life. Even though I could draft a spreadsheet and integrate statistics like no one else could, I was bored. Excruciatingly and utterly bored.

I didn't realize my true passion in life until I started baking "Fuck this major" cupcakes to cope with an intense tax law class. I'd brought them to a study group and they were devoured by my classmates in seconds, so I made more. Then I started branching out and making other things.

At first, I mastered the simple treats—different cupcakes, cookies, and brownies. Then I started to attempt the more intricate recipes: frosted éclairs, upside down sorbet style crescents, stuffed cream waffles.

The more I baked, the happier I became, but it wasn't until my mom brought it to my attention one day that I actually considered taking it seriously. I'd made her an orange soufflé for Christmas and she loved it so much that she took pieces of it over to her neighbors—demanding that they try it. She even called my then-boyfriend over and asked him to have some, to which he said, "Hmmm. It's edible."

Still, I'd realized my love for the culinary arts far too late. So, instead of switching majors, I remained in the business school and whenever I had free time, I stole classes from the number one culinary school on the beach: Wellington's Culinary Institute.

Every Saturday and Sunday, I went downtown and sat in the very back of the classroom—taking notes like I really belonged there. On the days that the class met in the actual cooking room— one stove per "paying student," I would simply pretend to be a high-schooler who was doing a research project.

It was what I was currently doing at this moment.

"Don't forget that you'll be graded on how you create the layers on your croissant." The professor said from the front of the room. "They'll need to be crisp, but not too flaky—soft, but never sticky…You'll also need to make sure your own personal design is something you've never created in this class before. Do not replicate any previous assignments or you'll receive an automatic demerit.

I watched as the woman standing in front of me stirred her batter and mixed in a few sprinkles of sugar. She tasted the dough and shook her head—sprinkling in even more.

"Hey…" I whispered to her. "Hey…"

She looked over her shoulder. "What?"

"You don't need any more sugar in that."

"How would you know, *thief*?"

I rolled my eyes. "Because you still have to fry it and coat it with a sugar blend, and that's before you even inject the sugared filling into it. If you use anymore, you'll give the taste-tester early onset diabetes."

She set down the bowl of sugar and got back to work, gratefully stepping over a bit so I could see the rest of her setup.

As I was writing down the list of ingredients, I felt someone tapping my shoulder.

"Yes?" I didn't look up. I was in the middle of writing down a brand of specialty dough. I was on the last letter when the notebook was snatched out of my hands and I found myself face to face with a woman dressed in all black. The word "Security" was etched across her chest in huge block letters and she was crossing her arms.

"What are you doing here today, Miss Turner?" she asked, pursing her lips.

"I'm uh…" I cleared my throat and sat up. "I'm here doing a book report."

"A book report?"

"Yes," I said. "A very important book report for my school. My *high school*."

"And what high school do you supposedly go to?"

"Pleasant View High."

"You go there even though it's been abandoned for fifty years?"

Shit. "I meant Ridge View…" I'd looked it up on Google earlier.

"All high schools are currently out for the summer. The last day was this past Friday." She snapped her fingers and motioned for me to get up. "Let's go. You know the routine…"

I stood up and took my notebook back, following her out of the room and into the hallway. "Is stealing lectures and taking extra notes in a class really a crime?" she asked. "Who am I really hurting here?"

She waved her key card over the pad at the door. "*Out.*"

"Wait." I stepped outside. "If I give you twenty dollars, will you go back and tell me what type of dough they're using for the specialty cronuts? Maybe I can give you my email address and you can send it to me?"

She slammed the door in my face.

Ugh... I tucked my notebook into my purse and heard familiar laughter. I looked up and realized it was the instructor from the "Understanding the Recipes" course.

"You think this is funny? I asked, feeling bold. "Kicking someone out of class?"

"It's hilarious." He laughed harder, looking at me. "And you weren't *kicked out* of class, you were removed because I saw you going in there this morning."

"You snitched on me? I thought you liked me...You don't normally snitch on me."

"I don't," he said. "But on test day, all bets are off. Can you not see the direct correlation between the times we have security remove you and the times we don't?"

I was stunned.

"Exactly," he said, patting my shoulder. "We all appreciate your passion, but test days are only for those who are actually paying tuition...I trust I'll be seeing you more often since you're out of college now, though?"

I nodded, and he laughed again, saying, "See you next weekend, Miss Turner," before walking away.

Completely honored by the "appreciate your passion" comment, I smiled and wondered if I could later get him to write me an unofficial recommendation for a few other culinary schools I was waiting to hear back from.

Maybe a letter from him would help me get a scholarship?

I glanced at my watch and realized I had three hours to get ready for the college I was actually paying to attend; my graduation ceremony was today.

track 3. all too well (3:42)

Arizona

Yep...*I definitely picked the wrong career path for my life...*
I was officially convinced that Reeves University officials had held a secret meeting dedicated to listing the many ways that they could make this year's ceremony the most boring yet.

Everything from the twenty minute organ prelude to induct the doctorates, to the thirty minute video that recapped the university's best features, to the fact that they'd booked five different speakers.

I'd sat through nearly all of them, scrolling through social media newsfeeds and twiddling my thumbs, but the fourth speaker of the day had definitely mastered the art of sounding as monotonous as possible. Every other line was "And then I remember," "I wish I'd known," or "I'm not making this up, kids...Hahaha."

There was never any laughter from the audience afterwards. Only silence. And snores.

I covered my mouth so I could yawn yet again, and the girl sitting next to me stretched out her arms and rested her head on my shoulder. Without my permission.

"Um   " I looked at her.

"Yes?" She looked right back at me.

"Um...Do I even know you? Why would you just lay on me?"

She blinked.

"No, really. *Why* are you laying on me?"

"Shhh!" She adjusted her position and shut her eyes.

I was tempted to jerk away and leave her hanging, but I decided to make the most out of the situation. I looked at the girl to my left—at the vacant shoulder that was calling my name, and leaned onto it.

Several minutes later, and once the speaker said he was "almost done" for the umpteenth time, my phone vibrated with a text from my mom.

"I'm sorry, hon, but I can't sit through another second of this. I got plenty of pictures of you walking across the stage, though! Oh! And I got a lot of you at the department ceremony earlier! I'll see you at home for your party! I'm making crab-cakes! Be there by seven!"

"You're my mother and you're leaving my college graduation EARLY? Really?"

"I actually wanted to leave TWO HOURS AGO, but because I'm your mother I stayed a little longer. Love you!"

I rolled my eyes, but I couldn't blame her. I texted, "Love you too, see you soon," and looked up into the arena. Some members of the audience were getting the exact same idea.

Hell, even some of the graduates were feeling the same way. The ones that still had the energy to get up, that is.

Before I could figure out what I wanted to do, my phone vibrated once more. Carter.

"Are you awake right now?"

"I am." I texted back. "I'm finding this speech quite inspiring. If you try to pay attention, you might learn something today."

"Bullshit. What is this guy even talking about?"

I listened to the speaker for a few minutes, honestly not understanding why he was now talking about a dead goldfish, but I pretended I did anyway.

"He's talking about taking chances, trying scary risks, and learning that just one of them is bound to pay off."

"You're so full of it, Ari. You should leave."

"I want to listen to the rest."

"Then I hope you have another way to get to your graduation party since I just saw your mom leave..."

"What? I don't remember rushing you out of YOUR college graduation. I sat through the entire thing!"

"I wasn't depending on you for a ride home ☺. You've got five minutes."

"I'll meet you there in ten." I gently pushed my neighbor off my shoulder and stood up.

"Sometimes, you just have to stay until the end," the speaker said a little louder, louder than he'd been for his never-ending speech. "I wish I would've stayed until the end of a lot of speeches when I was younger...I definitely wished I would've listened to the entire speech at my college graduation..."

What? I turned around, looking to see if he was not-so-subtly referring to me.

He was. He nodded and gestured for me to return to my seat.

"You never know what you'll miss out on..." he said.

I took a step back.

"This could be the most important speech of your life..."

I took another step back.

"And you might regret it for the rest of your—"

I turned around and rushed out of the room, hearing the laughter and applause of my classmates behind me. When I made it to the hallway, I looked back to see other students following my lead and joining the exodus.

College was officially over...

I took off my cap and gown and met Carter in the parking lot. "Since you made me leave early, you have to stop at Gayle's before we go to my graduation party."

"Do we have to sit inside?"

"I'm shocked you even have to ask…" I got into the car and he let the top down on his black Camaro—quickly speeding away to the diner.

Gayle's was the number one waffle house and sweets company on the beach. It was so popular that the company bought mobile-store trucks and drove them around campus during its season.

The menu wasn't anything special; it was beyond simple with its typical home-style American breakfast fare. What set it apart from anywhere else was the 1950s atmosphere and the undeniable this-shit-is-the-best-I've-ever-had-in-my-life waffle recipe. For years, the locals jokingly accused them of using crack in their batter to get people to come back so often, so the owner started boxing the batter in tins with the word "CRACK" written right on front.

Gayle's was also the only restaurant that had a ten page menu solely dedicated to their desserts, and they added new options and concoctions every week.

I'd pulled countless all-nighters, hosted several dates, and even held a birthday party there before. But no matter what, it was where Carter and I met up whenever life veered left and we needed to talk, or whenever there was nothing else better to do.

We met there so often that sometimes his other friends would simply show up if they needed him instead of calling him on the phone.

"Let me guess," the waitress rolled in front of us on her white skates as soon as we entered. "A Belgian waffle with vanilla yogurt and strawberries—with a sprinkle of chocolate chips for one order, and a waffle tower with chocolate yogurt, peanut butter, and a sprinkle of Oreo chips and candy on the side for the second order?"

We both nodded. We ordered the exact same thing every time we came here.

"Have a seat," she said. "I'll be right with you."

We took a seat in a booth by the bay windows—in perfect view of the tourists who were starting their annual takeover of the beach.

"I'm going to miss this so much…" I said. "If I don't get into anywhere else soon, I'll have to accept the offer from that culinary school in Cleveland. I don't think they have a beach, though…Or a restaurant that's similar to this one."

"They don't have much of anything. It's *Cleveland.*"

I laughed. "Just try not to rub it in since you're lucky enough to be staying here for law school."

"Don't worry. I'll be sure to send you ocean-view pictures every day."

"Here you two are." The waitress set down our orders and I swiped a spoonful of yogurt from Carter's plate.

"Ugh!" I swallowed it. "How can you eat that? The words 'chocolate' and 'yogurt' should never be allowed anywhere near each other."

He swiped a spoonful of my vanilla yogurt in return. "It's not like vanilla is that much better. There's no flavor in that whatsoever."

I shrugged and picked a few Oreos from his toppings cup while he picked a few strawberry chips from mine.

As I was stealing one of his peanut butter swirls, a few members of his college basketball team walked inside—super loud and obnoxious. Spotting Carter, they immediately walked over and shook his hand—asking a few brief questions, leaving Carter plenty of room to congratulate them on a hard fought season. Plenty of time for them to reminisce on his short-lived, yet high-profile freshman season.

The team had actually been quite terrible this year, posting the worst record in all of college basketball. And although his former teammates would never say it to his face, I'm sure they wondered if he'd lied about his diagnosis years ago, if he used his sudden ACL injury as an excuse to walk away from everything.

"Do you miss it?" I asked, after they'd said their goodbyes.

"I miss the groupies."

"You still have groupies. Just a different type."

"Well, in that case…" His eyes followed the team out of the store. "I never did appreciate other people unloading their expectations onto me when I had my own. So, no. I don't miss being a part of that at all."

"Totally understand. Speaking of which, when it comes to things we miss and don't miss…" I took out my phone and pulled up my secret "Long-term Relationship Compatibility" spreadsheet. I never told Carter it actually existed because I was sure he'd find a way to get me to delete it.

"What is one thing you wish you could've done differently in regards to your relationship with Emily?" I asked.

"I wish I'd never met her."

"Come on…" I started to type. "This always helps me know what not to do in my next relationship, so I'll go first. In me and Scott's case, I could've tried to talk to him about my reservations about intimacy a lot sooner."

"No, you could've tried *fucking*."

"And you could've tried *barking*." I snapped. "Maybe then Emily's meowing wouldn't have seemed so weird if you'd given it a chance."

"Oh?" He laughed. "Did I just touch a nerve? Are you that sexually frustrated?"

"No." I tossed a gummy bear at his face. "Although, it would be nice to have some amazing sex before I leave for culinary school."

"Then have some. I can help you with that."

"*What?*" I gave him a death stare. "Not with you. Are you out of your mind?"

"I'm definitely not talking about sex with me." He stole my last bite of waffle and stood up. "You wouldn't be able to handle me..."

I rolled my eyes. "Please!"

"Seriously though, I don't have much to do outside of work for the next few months," he said, "so I'll help you find a guy—or two or three, just for sex. As a matter of fact, we'll start the search tonight right after your graduation party."

"Are you sure you won't try to convince me to leave that early, too?"

"Not unless you somehow manage to make me fall asleep." He laughed and pulled me up, leading me out of the store.

As we sped back across the pier with the sun setting behind us in the distance, I realized I was already starting to miss this part of my life.

———

Later that night...

I stuffed one last piece of a cupcake into my mouth and gave my mom a hug. "Thank you for throwing me this party tonight."

"Anything for you." She hugged me back. "Wait a minute. Where is Scott? Is he coming by later?"

"Yeah, um...We didn't work out."

"Aw, sorry, hon." She gave me a look of sympathy. "You'll find someone better."

"I can only hope." I looked outside the window where the rest of my family was busy taking down lights and table settings. "What do you need me to clean up?"

"Absolutely nothing," she said. "I threw this party for you, so you don't have to help at all. Go out with your friends and enjoy the rest of your night."

"Who are you and what have you done with my real mother? The one who has OCD and insists that everything be cleaned within half an hour or less?"

"Hurry up and get out of here before I change my mind." She laughed and shooed me into the living room, where a few of my classmates were gathering their things and leaving.

On the couch, my former study partner for Logistics, Tina, was running her hand up and down Carter's arm. Not being subtle at all, she was blushing every other second and smiling the next.

"I'd love to talk to you sometime..." she said to him, biting her cherry red lip.

"I'd love to talk to you, too." He gave her that stupid, charming grin that apparently had an effect on every woman except me.

I walked around the room and individually thanked all of my classmates for coming, taking a few last selfies with them before they disappeared. I was about to thank Tina, but she suddenly leapt up from the couch and grabbed my hand—pulling me into the guest bathroom.

"Are you in need of a tampon or something?" I asked, confused. "They're in the bottom left drawer."

"No." She smiled. "I wanted to ask you something about your friend."

"Carter?"

"Yeah." She lowered her voice as if he was actually in earshot. "Would you be mad if I went out with him?"

"Why would I be mad?"

"Because, I mean...I personally think you two have probably done stuff in the past and there are some hidden emotions on your part, so—"

"There are no hidden emotions on my part." I cut her off. "And we have never even so much as kissed. We've barely even hugged...How long exactly have you thought that about me?"

"That's not the point." She waved off the topic. "The point is, I want to go out with him and I want to make sure it is okay with you since we're friends."

We were not friends. We were *study partners*.

"It's more than okay with me," I said. "You don't really need my permission. How about asking him out and not me?"

"I heard he has a huge cock." She lowered her voice again. "And that he's into really dirty and intense sex…Is that true?"

"How the hell would I know?"

"Oh, come on " She gave me a pointed look. "There's no way you've never copped a feel of his dick or given it a second look…"

"I haven't."

Trying to catch me in a lie, she tried the example approach. "He doesn't even go to our school, Arizona. Yet, I see him on our campus all the time."

"Are you aware that he's dated quite a few girls from our school before? That's another very good reason for that…"

"So, just to be one hundred percent sure, you're telling me that you two have never sampled each other?"

"Did you really just use the word 'sampled' in a sexual context?" I couldn't believe this. "Look, he and I have never had sex, let alone *sampled* each other, and you can trust me on this. You can also trust me saying that we *never, ever* will."

She looked at me for a few moments, as if she were trying to determine if I was going to somehow take everything back, and then she smiled. "You are too cute!" She hugged me—literally wrapped her arms around me and squeezed me so hard I started to cough. "Quick question, though…I figured you would know. What's his favorite color?"

"Blue, sea blue."

"Good to know." She winked at me as she opened the door. "I'll keep that in mind for what color thong to wear under my dress whenever he takes me out.'"

There wasn't an eye roll worthy enough to use for that so I simply smiled and followed her back out to the living room, waiting for her to say a few last words to Carter. She gave him her phone number, whispered something that sounded like, "I can't wait to fuck you..." into his ear, and gave him one last sultry look before leaving.

"Good party," Carter said, shutting the door behind her. "What part of the house do you have to clean up before you can leave?"

"None. My mom said I didn't have to help. She said I should just enjoy my night."

"There's no way she said that." He leaned against the wall. "Tell me so I can help you clean whatever it is. If we hurry up and get it done we can start your sex victim search long before last call."

"I was being serious, Carter!" My mom called from the kitchen. "You both can get out now!"

He didn't question it any further. "Bar crawl?"

"Absolutely." I walked outside and hopped into his car, changing the radio station and answering a few of his questions about Tina.

As we searched for a parking spot near the pier, I prayed to the Best-Friend-Gods that if he changed his mind and decided to get serious with Tina (or anyone else this summer, for that matter) that she wouldn't turn out to be another Emily. I couldn't handle another one of those...

Being his best friend was already tricky territory. All of his girlfriends automatically became suspicious when he introduced us. They smiled at me when he was looking, and glared at me behind his back. And, whenever he was on the phone with me, he always had to go out of his way to say, "No, really. She's just my best friend..." halfway through the conversation. Usually more than once.

There was almost always an ultimatum in his relationships, too: "Are you dating Arizona or ME?!"

Yet, since we're indeed "just friends"—just goddamn friends (why couldn't people see this?!), I had no issues with him falling back or not talking to me as much, because months later, the results were always the same: Another breakup. Another late night phone call to discuss what did or didn't go wrong. Another brief break until he found the next crazy.

In fact, sometimes I wished I could sit with his next girlfriend and say, "Hey, before you start thinking about doing anything stupid and accusing him of something that has never, and will never happen, here are a few facts that will probably ease your mind: 1) I'm not attracted to him. AT ALL. I don't get what all the hype is about, sorry. 2) I'm not interested in "fucking him." AT ALL. I've had enough great sex to keep me satisfied, and when I'm not with someone, my vibrator serves me just fine with fantasies of celebrities. NOT HIM. #Truestory. And 3) He once saw me naked at a pool party when we were eighteen and begged me—fucking *begged* me, to put my clothes back on. ASAP. So, yeah. He's not attracted to me either. Can you promise not to make any accusations about the two of us now?"

Of course, I was sure that scheduling a sit down with a potential girlfriend would lead to more issues instead of alleviating them, so I just went along for the train wrecks—hoping he would one day find someone who wasn't a psycho.

"Hey, Ari?" Carter waved his hand in front of my face minutes later.

"What?"

"Do you plan on getting out of the car tonight? He opened my door. "Or have you decided that you'd rather handle your pussy with your fingers for the rest of the summer instead?"

I rolled my eyes and got out, following him inside of Margaritaville.

I ordered the weakest beer they had to offer and surveyed the room. "If this whole casual sex guy thing doesn't work, do you think I'll find my one hundred-percent guy before I go off to Cleveland?"

"I highly doubt it." He smiled, leaning back against the wood. "You have three months until then, and you make guys wait for at least eight before telling them you've changed your mind."

"I'm being serious." I punched his shoulder. "It would be great to meet a nice, down to earth guy and feel like everything is perfect and right at once, you know? To have all of those right vibes and feelings upfront, so I wouldn't even have to worry about how it'll turn out in the long run."

"You're talking about insta-love?"

"I'm talking about love at first sight."

"That shit doesn't exist," he said. "Any relationship built solely on instant attraction is a recipe for failure. Trust me, I'm the prototype."

"You're the prototype for being a man-whore." I sipped my beer. "It's not the same thing."

"If I was a man-whore, I wouldn't have had six girlfriends over the past two years. *Six*, Ari."

"Six girlfriends, five one night stands, four "There's some girl in my bed and I don't know her name" mornings, three "Holy fuck, that sex was terrible" nights, and one—"

"Partridge in a pear tree?"

"No. One 'Please, Ari, come and get me.' But that was a very close guess."

"I didn't know you were keeping count…"

"Only because you make it too damn easy."

"I'll keep that in mind." He rolled his eyes. "Hey, look over there." He pointed with his straw. "What about that guy? He looks like he'd be into a few nights with you."

I spotted the guy he was talking about: He was dressed in a short sleeved white shirt and khakis that complemented his beige shoes.

"He's cute…" I looked him over again. "I don't think he's my type, though."

"He's more than your type. He looks like he hasn't fucked anyone in years."

I laughed. "No, thanks. What about that guy?" I pointed to a guy dressed in all blue.

"I thought you hated sneaker-heads."

My eyes roamed down to his shoes and I shook my head. After dating a sneaker-head, I knew those were the type of exclusive shoes that could only be worn by one.

"Oh, wait a minute..." Carter said, smiling. "Looks like you have an admirer. Look to your left."

I slowly turned around and spotted a guy in a black shirt and jeans smiling at me. He tilted his head to the side, as if he was trying to figure out the relationship between me and Carter.

I immediately scooted away and the guy smiled, shooting me a short wave.

"Go talk to him," Carter said.

"Shhh! Stop talking to me! He might think we're together..."

"He won't if you go talk to him, Ari. *Jesus...*"

I hesitated, still looking at the guy, and the next thing I felt was Carter pushing me out of my seat.

"Go." He shooed me away. "It's not like you're making me look appealing to anyone either."

I shook my head at him and walked toward the guy in the black shirt, blushing as I stepped closer. He looked ten times better up close.

"Hi..." He smiled a set of perfect pearly whites.

"Hi..."

"I'm sorry for staring," he said smoothly. "Did your boyfriend send you over here to tell me to stop?"

"He's not my boyfriend."

"Glad to hear that." He smiled again and extended his hand. "I'm Chris."

"Arizona."

"Nice to meet you…" He gently caressed my knuckles with his fingers. "I'm actually only here to take a few of my drunk friends home, but…I'd love to call you tomorrow and maybe meet up somewhere this week? Somewhere quiet and private?"

I nodded, slightly speechless at the way his simple touch was making me feel.

"Can I have your number, Arizona?" He slowly let my hand go and pulled his phone out of his pocket.

"It's 555-9076…" I managed to pull my phone out without taking my eyes off his. "Yours?"

"The number that's currently calling you." He grinned as my phone rang with the unknown number. "I'll definitely call you tomorrow." He looked me up and down as he stepped back. "It was very nice meeting you."

"Nice meeting you, too." I stood rooted to the ground until he disappeared into the crowd, and then I made my way back over to the bench.

"So?" Carter signaled to the bartender to close his tab. "How'd it go?"

"Good, really good. We only spoke a few words to each other, but he's going to call me tomorrow." I felt like a giddy little girl. "I literally felt something when he touched me—something strong."

"It's a pretty bad sign if he's already given you an STD."

"You are so terrible!" I laughed. "Did you find any future victims while I was gone?"

"Within the span of two minutes? No, but I realized we need to get you a few more dates tonight if we're going to guarantee that you get laid at some point this summer." He set a tip on the counter and clasped my hand, pulling me through the crowd and outside. "We need to go to a few more bars."

"What? *Why?* I just got a guy, a guy who has already promised to call me tomorrow and made me feel a genuine spark when he only touched my hand. Did you not hear any of what I said back there?"

"That was one guy, Ari." He shook his head. "One. Who knows if he'll really call you tomorrow? You trust him just because he said he would?"

"Well, yeah…"

"So, you'll believe anything a complete stranger says to you?"

"There was a spark, Carter…A genuine he-is-definitely-going-to-call-me spark."

"You need at least five other options." He unlocked the doors to his car and motioned for me to get in. "That's the biggest problem you have now. You need to actually date around and stop pinning all your hopes on the first guy that you supposedly feel a spark with."

"I don't always do that…I at least wait until he kisses me first." I laughed. "I'm a pretty good judge of kisses, you know. I can tell a lot about a guy from the way he uses his mouth."

"I'm sure you can." He revved up the car and sped down a few blocks toward a more popular bar. "You have stars in your eyes right now over a potential phone call. I'd hate to see what you look like after you get kissed."

"I'll record it one day and send you the video."

"Please don't." He looked over at me, laughing as he found a parking spot. "If it's anything like you looked after meeting that guy in there, I never want to know. Now, get out of the car before you start staring into space, so I can show you how to get exactly what your pussy needs."

"Really, though? Have I ever told you how deep you are?"

"No." He smiled as he got out of the car. "But that's only because you and I have never fucked…"

fifth grade

Carter

Dear Carter,

I don't care what you say about Dawson Meade the 3rd. He will be my first kiss and he will NOT care about my braces. He will fall in love with me and ask me to be his girlfriend. And then you will be jealous because you will still not know what it fills like to be kissed.

I'll let you know how it goes after school.

Sincerely kissed,

Arizona

Dear Arizona,

I do not care about your first kiss, but you should know that Dawson is lame and he will kiss anyone. I saw him kissing hisself in the bathroom mirror last week. Trust me, he will care about your braces. They are still not pretty.

And I will not be jealous because I'm getting my first kiss from Rachel Ryan today. She said we will do it like the French.

I will let YOU know how it goes after school.

Sincerely FIRST kissed,

Carter

Arizona balled up my note and rolled her eyes at me as the bell rang.

I closed my notebook and followed her to her locker, where we always met after school.

"Are you ever going to get those braces out of your mouth, Ari?"

"Why do you care?"

"Because I don't want to hear you cry when no one but Dawson wants to be your boyfriend...It's because of your braces."

I'd thought they couldn't get any worse, but sometimes she stuck colored rubber bands in them so she could eat. Sometimes I told her she should just starve.

"Did you and Rachel pick a meet up spot?" she asked.

"Yeah, we're going to meet at the tree outside the gym. What about you and Dawson?"

"We're going to do it in the parking lot behind the football team sign," she said. "Do you really think he'll care about my braces?"

"Depends....Do you really think Rachel will care about my hair?"

"What's wrong with your hair?"

"Last week, you told me it was itchy."

"It *was* itchy." She closed her locker. "Because you fell asleep on my shoulder."

"Oh yeah..." I remembered. We'd both got detention after school last week for passing notes during science class. And, as usual, whenever we got sent there together, I used her shoulder as a pillow.

"Ari, do you think we should..." I paused. "Do you think we should..."

"Do I think we should *what*?"

"Like...Since we're both getting kissed today, do you think we should test out the kiss first? On each other? That way we can be honest and fix whatever needs to be fixed?"

"I was actually going to ask you the same thing…" She let out a deep breath. "If we do that, then we both won't be so nervous when it's time."

"Okay, cool. Follow me. "I motioned for her to follow me down the hallway. I looked both ways to make sure no one was coming, and then I opened the door to the janitor's closet and pulled her inside.

She set her books down on a ladder and I locked the door.

"So…" She looked really nervous. "How should we start?"

"Well, first…" I stood in front of her and made sure our shoes were touching. Then I did the thing I always saw my dad do whenever he kissed my mom—tucked a strand of hair behind her ear.

"And now, we'll kiss on three." I cleared my throat. "One…"

She shut her eyes and grabbed my hands.

"Two…"

"Wait! I forgot something!" She pulled a tube of lip gloss out of her pocket and glided it across her lips. "Now, you can count."

Ugh! Girls…

I rolled my eyes and started over. "Okay, starting again… One…Two…" I shut my eyes and leaned forward. "Three…"

We pressed our lips together and let the seconds pass, waiting. Waiting for something.

It was nothing like the movies. Nothing was happening at all.

"Um…How long are we supposed to stand like this, Carter?" Ari asked, her lips still touching mine.

"I don't know…Maybe five more seconds?"

"Okay…Cool…"

I softly counted to five and stepped back.

"So…" she said. "Did you notice my braces? Were my lips too glossy?"

"No to the braces, but make sure you put on the gloss before you get to him. How about me? When my forehead touched yours, was it itchy?"

"Nope. It felt normal, but when you kiss Rachel, just count to yourself and not out loud."

"Got it." I grabbed her books and handed them to her. I unlocked the door and twisted the doorknob, but it opened before I could push it forward.

"*What the!*" The school janitor, the man who made us help him clean up sometime during detention, looked back and forth between me and Ari. "You know what? When it comes to the two of you, I don't even want to know. Get out. *Now.*"

"We weren't doing anything!" Ari snapped.

"Then hurry up and get out of my closet before I tell everyone that you did."

We both rushed out of there and went our separate ways— she to Dawson and me to Rachel for our very first kisses…

track 4. sad beautiful tragic (4:13)

Carter

"Ladies and gentlemen," the dean of Political Science spoke into the mic, "please welcome our last honoree of the night, Carter James!"

There was a loud applause as I walked onto the small stage and accepted my award—a silver plaque with "Student of the Year," etched across its front.

Tonight was the private post-graduation ceremony for the top students in my major. For whatever reason, the officials thought it would be a great idea to have it several days after all the other departmental graduations. They also thought it was smart to have it on the roof of a famous hotel, so those of us who got bored could easily stare at the beach in the background and look like we were paying attention.

"Thank you all so much for coming out to honor the top twenty students in our department," the speaker continued. "We'll also have you know that each of the students we honored tonight has scored a 177 or higher out of a perfect 180 on the LSAT."

More applause.

I looked at my watch.

"Help yourself to plenty of the gourmet dessert before you leave, and please be sure to keep in contact with us as you start your exciting careers in the law!"

When another round of applause began, I stood up and headed toward the dessert bar—to say goodbye to the few classmates I actually talked to during undergrad.

"Well, if it isn't Carter James..." A grey-haired man stepped in front of me, blocking my way. "What an interesting transition you made, huh?"

"Excuse me?"

"Superstar athlete to superstar student." He smiled, looking at my right leg. "It's too bad you got injured. I think the team definitely would have gone places if you'd never gotten hurt. Supposedly..."

I clenched my fists, somewhat grateful that I was wearing a suit; the fabric was less than forgiving if I needed to punch someone.

The man didn't wait for a verbal response, he continued talking—confirming what I'm sure every sorry ass fanatic on this campus wondered from time to time. "You don't think you should've gone to another doctor for a second opinion? The doctor you went to wasn't the best one. The school even offered to send you to New York to get tested. They also offered you rehabilitation, didn't they?"

"They did."

"I mean, don't get me wrong. Making the Dean's List every semester and scoring a 177 or higher on the LSAT—"

"I scored a 180."

"Right." He cleared his throat. "Well, that's impressive, son, but you could've gone places. Michael Jordan played in a pivotal playoff game with the flu. Hell, Willis Reed—one of the greatest centers of all time—played with a broken thigh bone. *Broken.*

Plenty of players come back from the type of injury you had, so I just don't understand why you couldn't give it a try."

"Are you done now?" I kept my fists low.

"What did your parents think about your decision?" He wouldn't stop. "Did you ever talk to them about it? I'm sure your father would've never—"

"Fuck you." I spat. "You don't know shit about me, and I don't care whether you don't understand a decision I made regarding my own life. Live your own."

"I'm just saying…"

"You won't be saying much of anything else if you continue," I said, narrowing my eyes at him. "Don't let this suit fool you."

He looked at me in utter shock.

"And for the record," I said, stepping back—giving myself some space, "Michael Jordan was a goddamn professional athlete when he played with the flu, I wasn't. Yes, Willis Reed was one of the greatest centers of all time, but he retired because he couldn't stop getting hurt, correct?"

He said nothing—just stared at me, so I walked away. I didn't bother addressing any of my classmates or stopping by the dessert bar. I needed to get home so I could be with people I actually wanted to be around.

I slipped into my car and turned the music all the way up, trying hard to put that asshole and his opinions out of my mind, but it was no use. Everything began to play in front of me like an antique film reel—frame dissolving into frame.

Five years ago, I didn't have to think about taking the LSATs or picking an academic track at all; I was being scouted as one of the top high school basketball recruits in the country. I was the "unexpected phenom" and "unbelievable talent" who'd only started playing basketball during my junior year of high school.

From the outside looking in, I really looked like I was passionate about it. I spoke to coaches from colleges all over the country, led my already-talented team to a state championship my senior year, but I was only using the attention as a deflection from my pain. Pain I hid all too well.

I spent extra hours every day at practice because I didn't want to think about anything, not because I wanted to improve my game. I pretended to be crushed and disappointed when we lost or when I missed a critical shot, but I didn't really give a damn.

I even felt slightly guilty about accepting a full athletic scholarship to South Beach University—knowing that I didn't want to play, and the media attention I was getting reached an all-time high freshman year.

Yet, four games into the season, I tore my ACL and my coping mechanism was ripped away from me within seconds. The media attention that was sudden and swift when it started, seemed to come to an abrupt stop.

Yes, the doctor had told me that I could play again with extensive rehab, that I could take six to eight months to heal and be just fine, but I asked him to write me a "should probably never play competitively again" diagnosis instead; I couldn't bear to live the life of a college athlete for another day. I had to force myself to find new ways to cope.

Since I had no family to call anymore—only memories could bring them to life every now and again, I relied on my friends.

Just friends.

There was Josh—my closest male friend, current roommate, and fraternity culture obsessed confidante who had an excuse for almost everything. There was my former teammate Dwayne—soon to be a professional athlete and first round draft pick, who still got me tickets to every campus basketball game. And of course, there was Arizona who'd stuck by me through it all—never letting me read what the papers were saying about the "Questionable Diagnosis," always there when everyone else had left me behind; she was my best friend—the ultimate person I could count on no matter what. And, for whatever reason, she was the only one who was standing in my kitchen when I finally made it home from the awards ceremony.

"You wanted to have a graduation party with just four people?" she asked as I came inside. "You know you could've easily gotten one hundred people here, and that's just me counting your adoring female flock."

"It just kills you that I'm sexually attractive, doesn't it?"

"It kills me that you can actually describe yourself as 'sexually attractive' without laughing at how ridiculous that sounds."

I smiled. "Would you like me better if I was modest?"

"I'd like you better if you were honest." She laughed, and Josh and Dwayne came inside the house at that moment—arguing about basketball stats as usual.

"You were serious about only inviting the three of us?" Dwayne asked, looking around. "No other girls but Arizona?"

"Is there a problem with that?" I asked.

"No." Josh shrugged, setting a bag on the counter. "After going to ten parties this week that were far too crowded, I think I'd much rather hang out in a small group tonight. Well, minus Arizona. I'm with Dwayne on that one. We can always do without her being here, and since I live in this place as well, I vote for her to go."

Arizona threw up her middle finger at him.

"I picked up a cake for you, Carter," Josh said, taking a six pack of beer out of a bag before handing it to me. "I figured you'd want an official one to celebrate tonight. Plus, I got some new alcohol that I need to use on a few of the slices later. Me and a few of my fraternity brothers want to run an experiment we saw on YouTube."

"Of course you do." I flipped the lid off the box, shaking my head once I read the lettering on the light blue cake. "Congratulations, it's a Boy?"

"They ran out of graduation cakes." He shrugged. "Better than nothing, right? Should I have gotten, Congratulations, it's a Girl?"

Arizona and Dwayne burst into loud laughter, and I couldn't help but laugh, too.

I grabbed my own six pack of beer and motioned for the three of them to follow me outside, past the backyard gate and to the beach. This was our last summer before we all would have to chase our own separate dreams, and I wanted to cling to the carefree life for a little while longer. The life where I could get away with being slightly irresponsible and all would be forgiven with an eye roll and slap on the wrist from the campus cops. The life where spending hours upon hours in a diner with friends and talking about absolutely nothing were the norm and not the exception, and a life where the beach was never more than a few blocks away.

Yet, as Arizona sat down right next to me in the sand—and began arguing with Josh as usual, I realized that something felt different about this summer already. But I couldn't tell exactly what it was yet...

———

A few days later...

I locked the door to my bedroom and read over my father's obituary for what must have been the millionth time—stopping on the words "He leaves behind a son he loved more than anything, his ex-wife (a woman who he always considered his "best friend") and a fiancée..." The "woman he always considered his best friend" was always the part that jumped out at me.

He'd disappeared somewhere between the sixth and seventh grade—in between one of my birthday parties and the start of puberty. There was no formal notice, no formal talk about why he was leaving; my mom and I woke up one morning—refreshed after our annual family vacation, and realized all of his stuff was gone.

The next time we saw him, he was on TV—heading some huge celebrity divorce case. The next time we saw him after that was in the newspapers—he'd just won one of the biggest class action lawsuits in the country. And the last time we saw him was at his funeral; his new, much younger fiancée had been drinking and lost control at the wheel.

To his credit, he gave my mother everything she *thought* she wanted in the divorce—alimony, child support, timeshares, and two vacation houses they'd bought together. He sent birthday and holiday cards like clockwork and every now and then he sent us flight tickets to visit him; flight tickets that never got redeemed.

For me, he called once a week—going down his normal list of questions. "How are you this week, son?" "How are your grades?" "Your mother says you joined a summer league basketball team. How's that?" "How is Arizona? Is she still your best friend?"

One day, circa seventh grade and tired of his bullshit, I cut off his checklist of questions and asked. "Why did you leave us?"

"What's that, son?"

"I said…" My voice didn't waver. "Why did you leave us?"

There was no immediate answer—only silence. After several minutes, I considered hanging up, but then he began to speak.

"I wasn't happy. We were only getting along for your sake… We were supposed to stay together until you reached high school, but I honestly…I couldn't do it, and I told her that, too…I should have been clearer and said that I just didn't feel the same as I used to, and I guess that's why we should've stayed 'just friends.'"

"That is the stupidest shit I've ever heard…"

"Watch your mouth." He snapped, his tone now glacial. "You asked me to be honest, so I'm being fucking honest…" He sighed and paused once more. "I never got to meet anyone new or find who I was outside of your mother. That's the problem. We settled for each other and we, in turn, stifled one another."

"You're blaming her for you leaving?"

"I'm blaming us both," he said. "No way can a man and a woman stay in love from childhood to forties and beyond. It's unrealistic."

"So, cheating on her with your secretary was the solution?"

Silence.

"How's school?" He changed the subject completely. "Arizona? Does she still have those braces?" And that was the last effort I made at attempting to salvage our relationship. Which was why I was quite surprised to learn what he'd left me in his will. In addition to a college fund, a trust fund, and a few of his investment portfolios, he'd left me a condo on the edge of the beach.

I vowed to never use it when it was awarded to me, and even contacted a realtor to put it up for sale. But, once I found out that the house was near South Beach University, I changed my mind and moved into it at the end of my sophomore year.

It was my much needed refuge from the hectic campus life and the beach fire parties, which was why I'd never invited more than three people over at a time. It was why I dreaded the idea of ever throwing a party here, but Josh was slowly wearing me down on the idea for this summer. He'd even begged me to have a business meeting with him about it at the end of my private graduation get-together the other day.

Sighing, I folded my father's obituary and returned it to the back of my desk drawer.

I stepped outside my room and headed into the kitchen where Josh and five of his fraternity brothers were sitting at the bar.

"You all wore suits?" I looked at all of their complementing grey and black suits.

"This is a business meeting, is it not?" Josh took out a folder.

"You're my roommate."

"And for that, I am forever grateful," he said. "And I think, to the best of my knowledge, we've gotten along pretty well for the most part. Right? I've never been late with the rent."

"There is no rent."

"But if there was, I would've never been late with it."

I rolled my eyes and took out a beer. This was going to be a long one.

"I also think," he said, continuing, "that I've taken great care of the backyard without you even asking. I've also made sure that the fridge stays stocked with water and protein shakes whenever we run out, and I make sure my company never overstays their welcome. So, with all of that on the table, I need you to give me three good reasons why you won't let us throw the party here."

"I can give you ten."

"I'm listening."

"One, we have neighbors on both sides, neighbors that don't really appreciate loud parties and have previously threatened to call the cops."

"We've already talked to them." He smiled. "They'll be away the weekend that we throw the party."

"*If* you throw the party." I countered. "Two, I don't want my things torn apart by drunk strangers."

"We plan to rent a U-HAUL overnight and place all of your furniture and TVs inside of it. We'll put it right back the next day."

"Three, you don't know how to count. You told me you were thinking about fifty people last week, but I saw the "secret" Facebook event this morning and it says three hundred people are coming."

"Three hundred seventy five." The guy next to him coughed.

"Yeah, so…" I took a long swig of my beer. "Hell no."

"Come on, Carter. Man…" Josh stood up. "It's not like you don't have the space, and it's not like everyone will be inside anyway. We have ideas to keep half of the people inside and outside."

"It's a no."

"You can't tell me you're not slightly interested in the thought of Jell-O pools and Slip N Slides. Or a wet T-shirt contest in your own backyard. This might be the last big party we'll ever have in our youth. We must protect our youth with memories like this, so when we're married with kids that we can't stand we can at least say 'Hey, once upon a time I actually loved my life' you know?"

"Do you ever think before you speak or do you just let everything come out randomly?"

"A little bit of both, actually," he said, smiling. "Don't make me beg you."

"Why can't you throw the party at your own fraternity's house?"

"Yeah...About that...." He cleared his throat. "After certain events that transpired last semester, Epsilon Chi is banned from throwing any parties on campus for the next five years."

"So you honestly think that shit gives me confidence in you throwing one here?"

"No, but I think if we do everything we said we were going to do a few minutes ago and offer you eight hundred dollars on top of that, you'd agree."

"You'd be absolutely right." I tossed my beer bottle into the trash. "Done deal."

He rolled his eyes and took off his tie while his frat brothers gave each other high fives. "Okay, since we have like two weeks to get everything together, would you mind helping us this weekend? We need to make multiple runs to pick up the tiki torches, some weed, and we have to start loading up on Jell-O and alcohol. It takes four people to hold the torch pieces though. They're supposedly fragile...and we kind of need to pick them up in a few days...So, unless you want to help us out by driving..."

"I don't. Ari can drive."

"Ari?" Josh's eyes widened. "Arizona *Ari?*"

"Is there another Ari we both know?" I looked at him. "Yes, that Ari."

"Dude, you've never let me drive your car."

"What's your point?"

"Ari is a girl."

"And you're a boy. Now that we've established what genders are, are we done here?"

"My point is, why does Arizona get to drive your car when I, your male best friend—best friend since junior year of high school—has to beg you to let me throw a goddamn house party …in a house we both practically share no less?"

I shook my head. Once a month, like clockwork, Josh brought up something about Arizona. Like a little child, he would ask why her and not him.

"You're not going to answer me?" Josh shook his head. "And you seriously have to wonder why everyone that comes around thinks you two are fucking?"

"First of all," I said, annoyed, "I don't give a damn what anyone else thinks. Even if we were fucking—which we're not, it wouldn't be anyone's business. Second of all, my car is a stick shift, and I would be more than happy to let you drive it if you knew how to drive one, but you don't. Do you?"

"Oh yeah…" He tried to save face. "Right. I forgot…Ari can definitely drive tomorrow. I have no issues with this at all. Glad we could have this discussion."

"Likewise. I want the eight hundred dollars a week before the party." I said goodbye to him and his friends, and returned to my room.

I opened my drapes and looked out at the ocean, at the people who were taking a late night stroll along the beach. Remembering that I was supposed to call Ari's friend Tina for sex later, I pulled out my phone and saw a message from Arizona herself.

"Get ready to eat crow! The Chris guy (Told you there was a spark!) is taking me out to the movies tonight. Take that!"

"You're just supposed to have sex with him, Ari. Not go on a date. (Not eating crow)"

"Yes, well…Some of us NORMAL people like to get to know someone first before having sex! Sorry we're not moving as fast as you and Tina are."

"Tina and I haven't had sex yet."

"Having problems getting it up?"

"Having problems getting across the bridge at rush hour."

"Well, I'm sure you'll succeed tomorrow. Meet up for waffles after my date? Ten-ish?"

"Eleven-ish."

"Great. See you there."

track 5. sparks fly (3:23)

Carter

Subject: Tina.

Want to know what she's saying about you behind your back?

—Ari

Subject: Re: Tina

No, but I would like you to hurry the hell up and get out here so we can get this over with. I thought you got off at noon today? (Why the hell do you still work here anyway? You barely show up and the manager hates you...)

Sincerely,

Carter

Subject: Re: Re: Tina

She's telling all of her friends that you have one of the filthiest/sexiest mouths she's ever experienced on the phone, and that she can't wait until you finally "fuck her brains out." (I honestly have no idea why I still work here...Give me a second to figure that out.)

Do I really have to drive?

—Ari

> *Subject: Re: Re: Re: Tina*
> *No comment on any of the Tina shit.*
> *Yes. HURRY UP.*
> *Sincerely,*
> *Carter*

I leaned back in the passenger seat of my car—continuing to wait on Ari with Josh and two of his fraternity brothers at the marina. I was hoping today would pass by quickly, as I wasn't sure if I could deal with the three of them for more than a few hours at a time.

"Did I tell you I started a private cannabis club in my fraternity, Carter?" Josh asked.

"No..." I immediately shot Ari another "Hurry up" email, and looked at him through the rearview mirror. "Did you already smoke too much weed today? It's kind of early for you, isn't it?"

"For the record, there's no such thing as smoking too much weed," he said. "Back to the topic at hand though, I have made it my personal mission to tell the new seniors that they are not to let my weed dreams die next year and to let my goals live on."

"Let me get this straight, you're happy about starting a secret club that promotes an illegal drug? Don't you want to be a governor?"

"Okay, first of all, weed is not a drug. It's an *herb*," he said defiantly. "This shit grows from the ground, just like a goddamn carrot."

"What about the side effects?" One of his own fraternity brothers countered. "The warnings?"

"What *warnings*? This herb may relax you and make you overwhelmingly calm, peaceful, and happy? Oh, yeah." He rolled his eyes. "The side effects are practically lethal. Weed cures glaucoma, helps the blind, and the only reason it's illegal is because the government knows that if they make it legal it'll be hard to tax because people might attempt to grow their own untaxable stashes in their backyard."

"Do you really believe this or are you actually high right now?" The other frat brother asked. "I'm honestly starting to worry about you "

"Ha!" Josh laughed. "Trust me, when I do become governor—after they expunge my record for all the shit I did freshman year, making weed legal in America will be my number one goal."

"Will cocaine be your number two?" I asked flatly.

"Screw you, Carter. Hear me out…"

I didn't bother. I shut my eyes and leaned back in my seat.

Never agree to help Josh with a party again. Never again…

"Look…" one of the frat guys whispered. "I would totally fucking hit that."

"Hell yeah." The other one laughed. "Easily a twenty out of ten."

"Nineteen point five…Half a point deducted for the smart ass mouth. I ran into her on our campus once."

"We're talking about looks, not attitude."

"In that case, I'll round up to fifty…"

The two of them laughed and I opened my eyes to see just who they were talking about, but the only woman I saw—the woman who was walking toward us, was Ari.

Dressed in a pink tank top and jeans, she was mindlessly walking—not a care in the world. Her long brown hair was waving in the wind, and for some reason I couldn't take my eyes off of her.

Nearly all of the men who were passing her by on the other side of the marina seemed to feel the same. They were doing double takes or staring at her in admiration for several seconds at a time.

"Yep…" one of the guys in the back said as she turned around to yell something over her shoulder. "And I would definitely hit it from the back."

Normally, I would've told him to shut the hell up, but my mind was currently perplexed by Ari—wondering why I'd never given her much of a second glance before today. Even in fourth grade (metal mouth included), I'd always thought she was cute— pretty even, but the woman walking toward us was more than that. Much more than that...

In fact, the closer she got, the more her features stood out in the sunlight: Plump and perfect lips, almond shaped eyes in a light hue of hazel, and a smile that was driving her backseat admirers somewhat insane.

What the fuck...

When she finally made it to the car, she tugged on her door's handle and groaned. "Really, Josh? I know this was you. Are you doing this to make a point?"

"Yeah," he said, leaning forward and unlocking the door. "You don't keep grown men waiting for you and if you say that you get off at noon, then you better make sure you get off at noon."

She rolled her eyes and slid behind the driver's seat, ignoring him as usual. "Since we're the only adults in the car..." she said to me as she cranked the engine. "Um...Hello? Why are you looking at me like that? Is there something on my face?"

"No..." I turned away and faced the windshield. "I was just thinking."

"About what?" She sounded concerned.

"I'll tell you later."

"You sure? You look really—"

"Um, hello?" Josh cut her off. "I hate to interrupt this daily episode of BFFs and their daily lives bullshit, but we have some party stuff to pick up."

"Whatever." She slowly pulled away. "Did I tell you that Carter is helping me to get laid before I leave for culinary school?" she said, smiling a perfect white smile in my direction. "He's a *real* friend. Unlike someone I know."

"I didn't grow up with you for over half my life, okay? I don't owe you anything. And as a matter of fact—"

I tuned out their voices. The two of them could argue for hours about absolutely nothing just because they wanted to. They always, thankfully, left me out of it for the most part.

And right now, I was more grateful than ever for their argumentative distraction.

I turned to my left to look at Ari again, hoping that the past few minutes were a mistake—that I was in the middle of a strange daydream. That there was no way I could be *this* attracted to her right now—no way I could want to tell her to pull over so I could taste her lips. Both sets of them.

The thoughts that were crossing my mind—ripping off that tank top—pulling off jeans shorts and spreading her across the top of my hood needed to be erased as soon as possible...

Holy fucking shit....

track 6. breathless (3:49)

Arizona

I pulled over at a gas station and bit my tongue to prevent myself from screaming. I wasn't sure how many more runs I could make with Josh and his frat brothers in the backseat, and if I heard him complain about my driving or heard the word "tiki torch" one more time, I was going to lose my mind.

I wasn't sure why Josh's fraternity was even attempting to throw another party. Granted, he knew how to throw a really good party, but he also knew how to break every rule in the book: Last year's "Unforgettable" themed party ended with half of the attendees running from the cops. The year before that—the "Legendary Experience," ended in a backyard fire, and I didn't want to even think about what he had on his mind for this year's "EPIC" event.

I shut the car off as soon as I put it in park and immediately got out, rushing inside the store to cool off. Literally.

Humming, I walked down the aisles and grabbed a bunch of junk since we still had quite a few trips to make. Twizzlers, Cheetos, and a couple of soft drinks for good measure.

Never agree to help Josh with a party again. Never again…

"You want anything from inside?" I texted Carter.

"Gatorade."

"What flavor?"

"Surprise me."

I grabbed a blue one and walked to the register, setting down my collection. I waited for the attendant to turn around and ring me up, but she didn't even look at me.

Her gaze was literally fixed on whatever was going on outside and she was mumbling to herself. "Oh my god…He is so perfect."

I cleared my throat to get her attention. Nothing.

I coughed a few times, even throwing in an "Excuse me?" but I got nothing.

Her manager, another woman, came through a back door and I expected her to say something to me, or at least be kind enough to ring up my stuff, but she joined the attendant's gaze fest instead.

"Jesus…" she said, making me finally turn around and look at whatever they were gawking at.

I knew it wasn't Josh. He was on the phone yelling about something that sounded like Jell-O. His fraternity brothers were laughing about something and pumping the gas. They were cute, but nothing drool-worthy, nothing gawk-worthy.

I tapped my chest, preparing to clear my throat again so I could get out of their self-imposed Twilight-Zone, but my eyes suddenly latched onto Carter.

I'd seen him shirtless a million times before, seen his blue eyes gleam in the sunlight many times more, but I'd never felt the slightest bit of attraction. Until now…

And at that moment, it wasn't "slight" at all…

With his six pack on full display, he was leaning against a different pump—looking off into the distance as beads of sweat trickled down his chest. He was flashing that charming smile he always used on an admirer across from him, but it was working on me from all the way over here.

He ran his hands through his jet black hair and I suddenly envisioned myself helping him with that, envisioned myself running my hands across his abs and lower—down to his perfectly defined "V" that trailed down to—

Oh. My. God...

I immediately looked away.

But then I looked at him again. I couldn't help myself.

How could I not have noticed this?

"Are you finally ready to check out or are you too busy staring at something out there?" The attendant finally addressed me, literally acting as if she hadn't been staring at him as well.

"Been ready." I stole one last glance of Carter and pushed all my stuff across the counter.

When she finished bagging my stuff, I returned to the car and waited for Carter and the other guys to finish stretching.

"Thanks for stopping, Ari." Josh sounded halfway genuine as he got in.

"No problem..." I said the same to his friends, and when Carter got back into the car, I couldn't help but take a closer look at him.

He is literally the epitome of sexy...

"You look kind of tired," he said softly. "Do you need me to drive?"

"No..." I shook my head and faced forward, cranking the engine. "I'm perfectly fine."

Holy fucking shit...

track 7. eyes open (3:59)

Arizona

I took a glass mug out of Carter's cabinet and placed it into a box.

"Is that the last one?" Josh walked over, picking it up.

"Yes, last one," I said and he immediately turned away and took it outside. Even though I told myself that I would go home after a day of running errands, I decided to stay and help box up Carter's valuables for the U-Haul truck. (Okay, and I also stayed behind to stare at him a little more so I could figure out what the hell was happening to me and my poor, confused brain.)

I looked over at Carter again and realized he was looking at me, too.

"Do you need me to stay and help with anything else?" I asked.

"I need you to go get some sleep." He looked concerned. "Everything's not going to get done tonight. You can come back tomorrow and help."

"I'm not tired," I said honestly.

"In that case…" Josh walked back inside at that very moment and pointed to a massive stack of boxes in the corner. "Could you organize all of the alcohol in those boxes by brand and type, please? And then when you get done, could you organize the rest?" He pointed to another stack that was hiding behind the doorframe."

"On second thought, I could use a break…"

"Don't break too long, then. The guys and I will be putting together a few of the torches outside if you need us, and while we work, I'll *think* about inviting you to our party."

I waved him away and walked over to the couch, collapsing on the rug instead of sitting next to Carter.

"Too tired to even make it to the couch?" He smirked. "Are you sure you don't want me to take you home?"

That actually might be a great idea right now

"Come here." He grabbed my arm and pulled me closer, positioning me between his legs. Then he began to gently massage my shoulders.

I shut my eyes and leaned back a bit, relishing the feel of his hands on my skin—trying hard not to focus on the fact that my nerves were currently on edge.

"How are things with you and Chris?" he asked.

"Things are pretty good actually. We went out for a run yesterday morning…He's a pretty decent kisser."

"So does that mean there's a high chance that the two of you will have pretty decent sex?"

"I think we'll have amazing sex." I swallowed as he pressed his palm against the back of my neck. "I also think it will be so amazing that it will make you jealous when I tell you all about it."

"Please don't." He let out a low laugh. "You should definitely invite him to the party."

"I did."

"Do I need to loan you my room to make sure you get the job done?"

"No…"

"Why not?"

"Because, although he appreciated the invite, he can't come. He works the night shift that day…How are things with you and Tina?"

"Nothing is happening," he said, kneading my shoulders one last time. "I still need to call her back."

"Any reason why you're dragging your feet?" I looked up at him.

"I haven't figured that out yet..."

Silence.

Neither of us said anything for a few minutes, we just stared at one another. He leaned down, moving a strand of hair away from my face and I felt my heart speed up, felt it thump and rock against my chest in a way it never had before.

"EPIC with a capital E!" Josh shouted, making us break away. "We now have the slogan for the party."

"Congratulations," Carter said, still looking at me.

"I knew you'd like it." Josh smiled. "Also, I need a quick reaffirmation from both of you for my friend Martin here." He pointed to the six foot guy who was standing next to him.

We exchanged confused glances.

"Please tell him that sex is the number one cause of ruin for all male to female friendships." Josh crossed his arms. "Before you answer, let me state the facts: One, if you sleep with the person who knows you best, you're creating a potential enemy. Two, once you have sex—the shit is never the same. Three, if you don't end up together, then you can't be friends. Ever. Do I sound like I'm making perfect sense or no?"

"It sounds like you're speaking from personal experience..." I stood up and nodded at his friend. "But...You do make a lot of sense."

"Perfect sense." Carter was suddenly at my side, extending his hand to Martin. "You should never sleep with your best friend. He's right. It'll never work out for the long term."

"But what if we both agree not to let it?"

"Nah..." Me, Carter, and Josh uttered the same thing in unison and laughed.

"Now that we've cleared that up," Josh said, smiling. "I don't mind you being around late tonight, Carter, but we're about to discuss some serious Epsilon Chi business, so could you kindly take your other half home? Her driving services were greatly appreciated today."

I rolled my eyes and tossed him a corkscrew. "I'll come back and organize the alcohol tomorrow. Although, I think I'll have to do them by color and not by brand since it looks like you stupidly tore off all of the labels."

"Not stupidly. Deliberately, my friend. They're for our new spin on the wet T-shirt contest."

"You disgust me."

"And you *arouse* me." He playfully licked his lips.

"Enough, you two   " Carter grabbed his car keys. "I'll be back. Please try not to burn down my house while I'm gone."

"*Our* house." He practically shooed us out the door. "And I'll do my best."

On the way home, Carter and I acted as if that moment near the couch never happened.

The night ended like it usually did in the summer after classes: Him pulling up to my house, waiting on me to go inside before pulling off, and then a late text a few hours later: "You feel like talking or getting a late dinner with me?"

ninth grade

Carter

Dear Arizona,
  You owe me twenty dollars.
  Sincerely,
  Carter

Dear Carter,
  Could you at least TRY to look like you're paying atten-
tion in class? And why are you passing me a note when we
both have cell phones?
  Annoyed,
  Arizona

Dear Arizona,
  I didn't see the twenty dollars you owe me in your last
note. Please respond with the appropriate funds. Thanks.
  Sincerely,
  Carter

Dear Carter,
  The only way I could possibly owe you twenty dollars
is if you had sex/lost your virginity this weekend. And since

*we both know you didn't, you can stop pretending like you
did. You can, however, send me twenty dollars for putting
up with this note writing bullshit.*

Grow up and use your cell phone,
Arizona

Dear Arizona,
Like I said....You owe me twenty dollars J
Sincerely,
Carter

She gasped as she read my final note, looking over her
shoulder and shaking her head. She sent me a text right before
the bell rang: "I'll see you after my Home-Economics class?
Your place?"

"Yours." I texted back. "My mom is having her therapist over
later. If you guys bake brownies again, bring me one."

"Done deal."

I floated through the rest of my day at school, not paying any
attention to anything that was happening around me. I even spent
an extra hour at test-prep tutoring—something I never did unless
I was bored out of my mind.

I walked the long way to Ari's house—stopping every minute
to look around at nothing in particular, but when I arrived she
wasn't there.

"Hey, there, Carter!" Her older sister, Ariana, ushered me
inside. "You want something to drink?"

"Water, please."

"Coming right up," she said, quickly pressing a cold bottle
into my hand. "You can go wait for Ari upstairs in her room if you
want. She should be home in a few minutes."

"No, thanks." I narrowed my eyes at her. "I'll wait here until
she gets back. Thanks to you, your mom thought we were up

there having sex last time I was here. Or do you not recall lying to her about that?"

"It was a joke." She laughed. "I honestly think we've all accepted that you two are just friends. Weird, strange, and way too damn close friends, but just friends."

"Not trusting it." I plopped onto the couch. "I've been scarred for life. Sorry."

She smiled and crossed her arms. "You know, I was just telling one of my friends about you two. I was telling her that although I think it's nearly impossible to be strictly friends with a guy, that I think you and Arizona are the rare boy and girl friends that will always remain strictly platonic."

"Thank you for your random thoughts," I said. "I was hoping that you would throw some my way today."

"Well, smartass, between you and me, have you ever had any non-friendly thoughts about Arizona? Has it ever crossed your mind that maybe one day she'll be your girlfriend? Or maybe—"

"You know what? I'm going to take you up on that room-pass now." I immediately stood up and walked up the stairs, ignoring her cackling laughter. I shut the door and sat by the window, resorting back to far more entertaining thoughts of sex.

It was ten times better than I thought it would be, and I couldn't wait to tell someone else about it. I wasn't sure how I was going to focus on anything else at school this week because I was going to need to have sex in my life a lot more often to cling to this current feeling.

"Can you stop smiling like that?" Arizona threw a pillow at my face. "You're giving it all away."

"So, you believe me now?"

"After seeing you sit there with that dumbass grin on your face for over five minutes?" She plopped onto her bed. "Yeah. I have no choice."

"Sorry, I can't help it." I walked over and plopped down right next to her. "It was so great."

"Who was it? Erica? Adriane?"

"Amber," I said. "We did it at her place Sunday afternoon while her parents were at a BBQ."

"How classy."

"We did it more than once, too."

"You're lying! There's no way…"

"Oh, young and unworldly, Ari…When thou hast experienced the wonder of the body, thou shall be able to effortlessly relate to the need and insatiability of bodily desires."

"So you do pay attention in Literature class?" She laughed and placed a wrapped brownie onto my chest. "I knew she was a pedophile…"

"She's only three years older than us."

"Whatever…" She rolled her eyes. "Who else knows?"

"No one." I hadn't told any of my guy friends yet—Josh was still serving out a suspension for skipping school last week, so Ari was my first call.

"What did it feel like?" she asked.

"Apple pie."

"I'm being serious." She rolled over on her side. "What did it feel like?"

"Good." I swallowed. "Really, really good…But…"

"But what?"

"You know how in all those dumbass chick-flicks you make me watch, when the actors have sex and they look into each other's eyes and act like their world has just changed forever?"

"Yeah?"

"It wasn't like that at all."

"Really?"

"Really…" I shrugged. "I mean, don't get me wrong, it's like the best feeling ever in life—especially when I first thrust inside of her and felt how tight her—"

"Ugh. Please spare me the grisly details…"

"Okay, okay." I laughed and turned on my side to face her. "It's really, really amazing, Ari. But if it's supposed to be anything like the movies, then I must be missing something."

"Or, maybe you did it wrong?"

"No." I laughed harder. "I definitely didn't do it wrong."

"What about in the pornos then? Was it anything like that?"

"You watch porn? Since when?"

"Since…a while ago." She pulled out her phone. "PornMD.com."

"No, no, no." I took her phone and shook my head. "You have to use pornhub.com. It links to all the best sites, and its way better organized." I typed up the website. "What category do you normally watch? Amateur?"

"Hardcore, actually."

"You're kidding me "

"I'm not." She looked genuine. "We watched a ton of them at Lisa Jane's party last month. I watch them like twice a week now. I think I might be addicted."

"A virgin addicted to porn?" I rolled my eyes. "I think I've heard it all now. You're just going through a phase."

She scooted close to me as I hit play on a video: "Double D Lila Gets Pounded by Huge Cock."

"Of all the videos you could've picked…" She sighed.

"This was under the hardcore category, thank you very much." I turned up the volume.

Onscreen, there was no attempt to even create a storyline. The blond model stripped out of her white T-shirt and spread her legs atop a desk as a guy wearing a "Vitamin D" shirt stroked his cock a few times.

"Can't wait to pound that pussy, babe," he said, winking at the camera. "You have such a beautiful and slick pussy."

Ari and I laughed.

Vitamin D grabbed Lila's hips and bent her over a chair, slapping her ass a few times before slipping his cock inside of her.

"Do you think her boobs are real?" Ari tilted her head to the side as Lila's breasts bounced up and down, as Vitamin D pounded into her again and again.

"Nope. They're silicone. See how the skin around the boob doesn't move? How they keep their perfect too-good-to-be-true shape? It's definitely silicone."

"That is hands-down, the worst explanation I've ever heard."

"It's the truth. Next time you take a shower just jump up and down in the mirror and compare how your boobs—what little you have of them anyway, move compared to hers."

"I'll definitely let you know. What about her butt?"

"Arizona! Carter!" Her mom called up the steps and I exited the site, handing the phone back to Arizona. "Both of you come down here and help me put up the groceries! And yes, Carter, you're required to help since you eat your fair share of them every week!"

I rolled out of bed and pulled her up.

"Okay, wait. I have a confession," Ari said, crossing her arms. "I'm insanely jealous that you had sex before me. There. I said it."

"I'd be jealous, too." I laughed. "But you want that whole Prince Charming-stars-in-your-eyes fantasy for your first time, remember?"

"Yeah, I guess."

"Just keep watching porn until you find the right guy in real life, and you better tell me when it happens."

"I will." She opened the door. "Always."

"But if it doesn't happen, I can always give you a sympathy fuck…That's what a true best friend would do."

She slapped the back of my head and pushed me out of the room. "If we ever did sleep together, *I* would be the one giving you a sympathy fuck…"

track 8. both of us (4:21)

Arizona

For the past few years, I've honestly tried my hardest to land a female best friend: Somebody I could get my nails done with, somebody I could talk to while obsessively discussing every detail of a date gone bad, and somebody I could point out a hot guy to and say, "Hey…I wonder how big his cock is…" with no judgment whatsoever.

Yet, every time I tried, one of three things happened: 1) The trial-BFF wanted to bring Carter everywhere with us just to get close to him, not me. 2) She was only using me for something school-related. (I still felt violated by trial BFF Carla, who apparently only wanted to be my study partner because I brought home-baked snacks to every all-nighter… "No snacks, no friendship") 3) She turned out to be Nicole, the girl who was currently standing in front of my full-length mirror.

Dressed in a thin white dress that stopped mid-thigh and left little to the imagination, she was flat ironing her hair for the umpteenth time, making sure it was absolutely perfect…for a house party.

We'd met in one of my business classes last year, and I thought it was such a good sign since we had the same boring major in common. Until she dropped out a month later and told me, "I was only taking that class to get close to that football player. Did you know he's going pro in the fall?"

Still, I clung to our fast-flame friendship—texting her small bits about my life, asking for hers in return. We did meet up to get our nails done every other weekend, and she never did judge me when I said, "I wonder how big his cock is..." because she wondered, too. But that's where her potential BFF qualities ended.

Even though she was nice and gave pretty sound advice from time to time, she was always flaking on me at the very last minute, always meeting some new guy she *"had* to experience." If we hung out for something other than nails or drinks, that usually just meant parties. No studying. No late night obsessive chats about guys. (I mean, although I could tell Carter anything and everything, I still wanted someone who could better relate from a female point of view).

"Why am I still trying?" I muttered under my breath.

"What's that, Arizona?" Nicole set down the flat iron.

"Nothing. We should probably leave soon, though. There isn't much parking at their place."

"Oh..." She looked over her shoulder. "You're ready to go and you're wearing *that*?"

I looked down at my pink tank top and khaki colored shorts. "Yeah. Why?"

"It's a party, Ari."

"A *house* party. There's no need to dress up like it's a real club."

"I couldn't disagree with you more," she said, walking over to my closet. "You've got way too many good options in here to show up looking like a hillbilly."

"Are you aware that your pink thong is showing through your dress right now? What little of a dress you have on, anyway?"

"Duh! That's the point!" She laughed and pulled a short red dress from my closet. "This is perfect."

"The last time I wore that, I was a freshman. I highly doubt that I could fit that tonight."

"Let's hope you can't!" She tossed it to me. "The tighter the better."

Holding back my words, I shut myself in the bathroom and took off my original outfit. I pulled the four year old dress over my head and smiled when it actually fit. (Well, if I sucked in my stomach a little.)

"How's this?" I stepped out for her approval. "Better?"

"A hundred times better…And it'll be two hundred times better when you let me do your hair and make-up. God, Ari! No makeup before going to a party? House party or not, you can't be serious…"

I bit my tongue once more and sat on the edge of the bed, letting her turn me into her personal Barbie. She dusted my eyelids with a shimmering shade of pink, plucked a few errant eyebrow hairs, and coated my lips in a deep, sultry red that complemented my dress.

She even somehow managed to use enough frizz control on my hair that she pulled it into a gorgeous high bun that sat perfectly centered on the top of my head.

"Wow…" I said, almost not recognizing myself in the mirror. "You're so good—no you're absolutely phenomenal with makeup, Nicole. Why haven't you ever pursued cosmetology?"

"Because if I pursue cosmetology, I won't meet any future athletes or CEOs in those classes." She laughed and hit the lights. "Let's go."

———

It took us over forty minutes to locate a decent parking spot when we arrived. It seemed as if Josh had invited every person he'd come into contact with because cars were hugging nearly every available space for five blocks down.

Ever the rebel, Nicole parked her car in the driveway of the house next to Carter's.

"What?" she asked, shrugging. "I left them plenty of space to park right next to me, and they're probably in bed anyway."

"Right…" I got out of the car. "You're not going to ditch me for some random guy tonight, are you?"

"Why would I? And why do you always ask me that?"

"Because you always ditch me for some random guy."

"It's never intentional." She smiled. "I plan on making sure we both have a good time tonight, so no, I will definitely not be ditching you."

I won't hold my breath…

"Five dollars ladies," the guy said as we approached the front door. "It's free if you're entering the wet T-shirt contest."

The guy standing next to him, a guy I'd seen here with Josh plenty of times before, laughed. "Arizona and her friend don't have to pay to get in. They're good…"

With that, the guy opened the door and let us into the party.

My jaw dropped the second I stepped inside. The house was now completely unrecognizable.

Dancing bodies packed the sparsely furnished living room and hallways; the kitchen had been converted into a wet bar where people were taking shots back to back, and tons of shimmering green and blue streamers were hanging from the ceiling.

As Nicole and I pushed our way through the crowd, I could hear people in the backyard chanting—counting down from ten.

Taking my hand, Nicole pulled me in that direction, out into the warm summer air.

"Whoa…" she said, looking impressed. "This is one hell of a party "

I couldn't agree more. The backyard was even more impressive than the inside. Those massive tiki torches were burning bright, standing in a huge semi-circle that spanned the entire yard. To the left, a guy dressed as a referee was calling on volunteers to battle inside a retractable pool of red Jell-O.

To the right, there was a makeshift dance floor with a separate D.J., and behind him there was a collection of bright yellow Slip N Slides that a group of bikini clad partiers were using to their full advantage.

We made our way down the deck's steps and walked past the Jell-O pool, over to a table of flashing neon lights that read, "BAR."

"What can I make for you ladies tonight?" The bartender asked. "The special tonight is three dollar Jell-O shots, but I'll give a two dollar discount if you lift up your shirts right now and flash me."

"You wish." Nicole laughed. "We'll take four shots of vodka. Each."

"Sounds good." He tapped the table with his fingers "That'll be thirty two dollars."

"Wait!" Josh rushed over, moving behind the bar. "Wait. You can't charge Arizona."

"Who's Arizona?"

"That one." He pointed his finger at me and narrowed his eyes. "She's my roommate's number one."

"So?"

"So, in exchange for him agreeing to let us throw this little party here..." Josh returned the dollar bills to Nicole. "She and her friend don't have to pay for any of their drinks tonight."

The guy shrugged and made the drinks while Nicole gave me a high five.

"Tell me, Josh." I crossed my arms. "Did you do that out of the kindness of your heart or were you forced?"

"I was forced. If it was up to me, I'd charge your ass triple."

"I'll be sure to drink all night then."

"Right..." He smiled and playfully pushed my shoulder. "I've got four of my guys running safety rides all night. Let me know if you and your friend get too drunk to drive."

"Thank you."

"Anytime." He stepped back, slowly looking me up and down with his eyebrow raised. He looked as if he wanted to say something else, but he settled with a "See you later" and walked away.

"Thank you very, very much!" Nicole winked at the bartender as he handed her a tray of red cups. "Let's go sit over there, Ari."

I followed her to a small wooden bench, and she set the drinks between us.

"Make sure you tell Carter I said thank you," she said. "Once again, your friendship with him comes in handy at just the right moment…Now, to take full advantage of your discount, we'll need to drink all of these back to back and then we've got to do four more."

"Eight shots within the same hour? Are you insane?"

"Not at all." She handed me a shot. "Live a little, Ari. Since you're not having sex and god knows the next time that'll happen for you, you might as well experience *something* in life that feels good. Alcohol would be more than a great start."

I tossed back two shots and winced, clenching my teeth together as the liquid burned my throat.

She handed me the other two cups, and as if she could read what was on my mind, she put up her hands in a fake surrender. "No, I'm not going to attempt to drive back tonight. We'll catch a safety ride at the end and I'll get my car tomorrow."

"Great." I finished off my shots and held my hand over my chest until the searing sensation went away.

"Ready for the next set?" Nicole asked, standing up.

"Oh, no. I have an early date with that guy Chris I told you about tomorrow, so I really shouldn't drink that much."

"If I was Carter, I'm sure you'd happily agree to drink more with me right now "

"If you were Carter, you'd know that I'm a super-lightweight."

"Well, thank god I'm not him, huh?" She pulled me up and tugged me over to the bar again. This time, instead of sitting down to drink the next set, we drank them in front of the bartender, and he even joined us for two of them.

By the time the eighth one had entered my bloodstream, I was feeling loose and overly happy. And I wasn't sure what came over me, but I ordered even more alcohol. Now unable to resist Nicole's whines of "But everything is FREE!" I downed several mixed drinks, nameless concoctions, and at some point, I was pretty sure I drank a shot straight out of her cleavage.

Shit...

"Slip N' Slide time!" Nicole yelled, pulling me across the yard.

"Yesssss..." I slurred, trying my hardest to walk in a straight line. "Slip...Slip N' Slide time..."

"Come on, Ari! Stop dragging your feet!"

"I'm not...I'm not dragging..." I stopped. "Whoa...." The ground was rotating beneath my feet and I was pretty sure the blades of grass were trying to jump up and cut me.

"Ari?"

"I think I need...to sit...too many drinks."

"Nah! You'll be good once you hit the water!" She linked her arm in mine and practically herded me to the line.

"Ladies first." The only guy standing in front of us turned around. "You two can go ahead."

"Thank you very much." Nicole batted her eyes. "Okay. You first, Queen Lightweight."

I took a step forward, kicking at a dandelion that was dancing on the ground. I tried to find my balance, staring straight ahead at the massive yellow tarp.

"You just run and lunge for it..." the guy said behind me. "You also have to yell 'EPIC' as you slide. Josh's rules not mine."

"If I do this," I said to Nicole, still trying to find my balance. "Can we sit down after?"

"Right after."

"Okay...." I slowly kicked off my sandals and made a run for the tarp, yelling "EPIC" as my body hit the plastic and slid faster than ever.

When I reached the end of it, I could feel a sudden blast of cold water being tossed onto me.

"Epic with a capital E!" The frat guys above me shouted. Before I could yell at them and ask what the hell they were doing, I looked over to the other tarp and realized that they were throwing buckets of water on everyone who did it.

Laughing, I let them help me up and waited for Nicole to take her turn. Of course, to garner as much attention as possible, she took off her dress—exposing a bikini that barely covered her Double D breasts, before taking the plunge.

The guys at the end shouted in loud appreciation as she stood up and adjusted her top.

"What?" she asked, smiling. "It's way more fun with a captive audience, don't you think? Want to go again?"

"Shockingly, hell yes."

We slid down the plastic over and over again—giggling like little girls each time, running over to the bar for more alcohol in between.

I gave no thoughts to the fact that my dress was soaking wet, that my once perfectly styled hair now resembled a mop, or that I was drunker than I'd ever been in my entire life. Also, no matter how hard I tried, I couldn't stop laughing.

"Okay, I think we should try to get dry now," Nicole pointed toward a bonfire that had just started. "I just overhead some guy saying they're doing free Skittle shots inside. They're also doing a power hour at midnight."

"Is that a good thing?"

"It's a *great* thing." She smiled. "They turn off all the lights so we won't have to guess much of anything if we see a cock we're curious about. We can just cop a quick feel for ourselves."

"You're ridiculous!" I burst into laughter as I took a seat in front of the fire.

The bright flames flickered and hissed, and as I held my hands out for warmth, I spotted Carter walking onto the deck.

Dressed in a black muscle shirt and dark blue jeans, he raised a red cup to me and Nicole before taking a long sip. Close by his side was Tina, and her eyes were completely glued on his body.

She was blushing and rubbing her hands against his chest, but he wasn't paying her any attention. He was looking at us. At *me*.

His eyes trailed up and down my body, taking in my soaked dress and messy hair, but it didn't look as if he was questioning it at all. Smiling, he looked me over one last time, and then he finally turned away to address Tina.

I watched as he gave her his usual "I know goddamn well that I'm charming the shit out of you" routine: A deep stare into the eyes, a light clasp of the wrist, and a few hushed and whispered words into the left ear that almost always led to an immediate blush. Watching him do those things normally made me roll my eyes, but tonight, I was envisioning myself in her place.

What is he saying?

My eyes roamed his body again and again—taking in the black tattoos wrapped around his sculpted right arm, his muscular chest, his mouth…And I seriously began to wonder how his lips would feel against mine.

Is he really into dirty sex? Would he have told me so if he was…?

"Are you checking Carter out?" Nicole asked, interrupting my thoughts. "Is that what you're staring at?"

"No," I said, lying. "Just thinking about something, and for the umpteenth time, Carter is like a brother to me."

"Brother-brother or stepbrother? Because if it's more along the stepbrother route, you should give it a try someday. How big do you think his cock is?"

Like he was any other random guy, I let my eyes drift toward his pants, but I stopped myself. I preferred to look at his lips instead.

As if Carter could feel me staring at him, he slowly turned around and looked in our direction again. He smiled at me and I blushed. Actually blushed.

Oh my god... "I've definitely got to get out of here."

"What's wrong?"

"Nothing, I...I just think I might be drunk."

"You *are* drunk."

You don't like Carter...You don't like Carter...There's no way you like Carter... I tried to keep my psychotic mind in check.

"Um, Ari?" Nicole asked. "Why does it look like you're about to get up and run away?"

"No idea...Can we please go inside?"

"Sure." She stood up and slipped her arm in mine, slowly pulling me to my feet. "You know, I would so sleep with Carter if he wasn't your best friend and liable to tell you all about it the next day."

"Gee, thanks..."

"You're totally welcome!"

Leading me across the yard like I was an elderly woman, she stopped each and every time I asked her to, and since that was at least ten times, it took us forever to make it back to the deck.

"Okay. Now, up the steps," she said. "Right foot, left foot... No, no, no. Your right foot, Ari. That's your left...That's still your left..."

"What's wrong with her?" The sound of Carter's deep voice made me look up.

"Nothing. She's just super drunk because she drank over ten drinks. You should've seen her do a body shot. It was epic with a capital 'E' indeed."

"She probably didn't eat enough before coming here, then." He slipped his arm around my waist and carried me up the remaining steps. "No offense, but as her friend, you should've known that she's a terrible hard-liquor drinking buddy. She's the perfect definition of a lightweight."

"I honestly had no idea..." Nicole's cheeks turned bright red in slight shame, but her eyes zoned in on Carter's lips. "Since I don't want her to go to sleep just yet, I was going to get her some water and have her dance off some of the alcohol. Care to join us?"

"In a minute, sure." His blue eyes met mine. "Are you feeling okay? Do you want me to take you home?"

If you do take me home, do you promise to have sex with me? I think I'd like to do that with you...Right now...

I silently chastised my mind's attempted response, grateful that it had at least had enough sense to send a signal for me to bite my lip so those words wouldn't come out.

"Ari?" Carter was still looking at me, waiting for an answer. "Do you want me to take you home?"

"No..." I managed, fully aroused by his touch—by the way his hand was rubbing my back.

"*Carter...*" Tina whined behind us. "Since she's okay now, can we go get another drink together? I don't want to go alone..."

He asked if I was okay and looked me over one last time before taking Tina down to the yard bar.

"You were right." Nicole said, opening the door to the house. "He's definitely like your big-brother."

I don't think I would ever want to sleep with my big brother...

The second I stepped inside, the mix of weed fumes, wasted alcohol, and body sweat were so strong that I felt like I was going to pass out.

To my surprise, Nicole retrieved a few bottles of water and patiently encouraged me to drink them before pulling me onto the dance floor.

White and red strobe lights were now illuminating the room, striking the walls with their brightness. And every few minutes, the DJ shouted "Get ready! Power hour is almost here!" over the bass.

With the alcohol still in control, I shut my eyes and swayed to the music. I even leaned forward, grabbing onto a pair of shoulders for support, but those shoulders moved away—making me stumble.

"Is that your way of asking me to dance?" Some random guy turned around and caught me before I could fall.

"Sorry..." I stepped back.

"No need to apologize." He placed his hands around my waist and steadied me. "Better?"

"Much...Thank you."

Several songs later, when I was finally able to distinguish the difference between the ceiling and the floor, I was able to dance without him holding my hips.

"All the single people scream!" The DJ shouted over the speakers. "It's power hour, bitches!"

I screamed my lungs out and danced to the techno beat—leaning my head back against random stranger guy's chest. I felt his grip tighten around my waist, heard him whisper something in my ear, but my focus was on the music.

"Hey, Arizona!" Nicole stepped in front of me, shouting and waving her hands. "Ari?!"

"Yeah?"

"This has been really fun, but I'm leaving now. Are you going to be alright?"

"Wait, what? You're leaving the party?" I yelled over the music. "I'll come with you, I just need to find my—"

"No, no, no..." She cut me off. "I'm leaving with a guy and we're going back to his place. Looks like you found someone to go home with, too."

"No, I'm just dancing..." The sober part of my brain surfaced and wondered if she honestly thought leaving me here alone was something a good friend would do. "I thought we were supposed to take a safe ride together?"

"We *were* until I found a guy, a very hot, I-was-dancing-on-him-and-felt-his-massive-cock-in-the-dark guy." She put her hands on my shoulders. "You'll be totally fine…Besides, Carter is here. He'll definitely make sure you get home okay. If you don't want to go home at the end of the night, the guy you're dancing with is really, really good-looking…Just saying." And with that, she left me in the same way that she'd left me a hundred times before.

I shouldn't even be surprised anymore…

Random stranger guy spun me around to face him and smiled. He leaned close and whispered into my ear, "You want to get out of here?"

"Like, together?"

"Yeah, babe." He smiled. "*Together.* My place?"

"Your place?" My brain still wasn't firing off enough logical neurons. "To have sex?"

"Um, yeah." He looked amused. "To have sex. *Good* sex…"

"No, I'm uh…" I shook my head. "I don't think I'm sober enough to have sex right now."

"Why do you need to be completely sober? I'm good at what I do, I'll make sure you feel more than satisfied when I get done with you…"

What the…

I immediately yanked my hand away from him and pushed my way through the crowd, heading straight for the bathroom. I knocked, waited for a reply, and when none came, I slipped inside and shut the door.

I turned on the cold water and splashed my face repeatedly, murmuring, "Sober up, sober up, sober up…." I gave myself another slap of water and heard the door opening.

"Hey!" I snapped, turning around. "I'm in here! Do you not believe in knocking first?"

"I do," Carter said, stepping inside. "I saw you come in here so I wanted to check on you."

"Oh." I continued splashing my face. "Thank you."

"Where's Nicole?"

"Where do you think?" I looked at him through the mirror, prepared to say something else, but I got distracted by his smile. *Has he always had dimples?*

"You should probably stop trying to force that friendship." He turned off the water and took a face towel from under the cabinet, pressing it against my wet forehead. "I personally think you can do much better."

"Well, I personally think you can do much better than Josh, but you don't see me complaining."

He laughed and pressed the towel against my cheeks and my neck. "Are you okay?"

"Yeah." I nodded. "I'm going to catch a safety ride later, but I think I want to dance for a little bit more…"

"I'll join you." He opened the door and followed me out.

To my surprise, the living room was even more packed now and the lights were a lot dimmer. Since we couldn't find a decent spot on the dance floor, Carter grabbed my hand and led me over to a corner.

He put his hands on my hips as we danced together, but unlike the numerous times that we'd danced before, my nerves were going out of control. My heart was racing a mile a minute.

I tried to act normal as the music shifted from chaotic to sensual, as he pulled me so close we were nearly lip to lip, but it was no use.

I wanted him to keep his hands on me, to touch me for the rest of the night.

"You look beautiful tonight, Ari…" he whispered against my mouth, letting his fingers caress my skin through the fabric of my dress.

"Thank you…" I breathed.

"Have you ever worn this dress before?" He tugged at its hem.

"Freshman year." I blushed and buried my head in his chest to prevent our mouths from getting any closer.

"Are you sure you're feeling okay?" he whispered into my ear, but I didn't answer. I was breathing in his scent, exhaling as he pressed his hand against my thigh.

"Ari?" he asked. "Ari?"

I ignored him once more, and instead of questioning it, he ran his fingers through my hair—setting my nerves on fire all over again.

A few songs later, when I'd convinced myself that my increased heartrate had nothing to do with the fact that Carter was still holding me close and touching me, I looked up at him.

"Why is the DJ playing slow songs now?" I asked.

"Would you like me to tell him to change it?"

"Yes…" I said softly. "Yes, I would."

The lights in the room dimmed even darker, to where I could only make out the outline of his face.

"It'll speed back up in a second," he said, his lips slightly brushing against mine. "He always slows it down before the next power hour."

"Right…" I felt his forehead touching mine.

The lights suddenly went black, and the next thing I knew, his lips were all over mine and my back was pushed hard against the wall. His tongue slipped into my mouth—demanding complete and utter control, and I immediately gave in.

Murmuring, I shut my eyes as he used his hips to keep me pressed against the wall, as he used one of his hands to slightly cup my ass.

He slid a hand under my dress and softly ran his fingers against my panty-line; in response, my arms went around his neck—my fingers threaded through his hair. He bit down hard on my bottom lip, so hard I moaned. But he didn't stop kissing me. He kept his mouth attached to mine, barely giving me a chance to breathe.

"Ah…" I let another murmur escape my lips, and he bit my lip again. Even harder this time.

"Alright, enough of this slow shit!" The DJ bellowed! "Power Hour, part two bitches!"

The strobe lights came on again, and Carter and I quickly tore away—panting and staring at each other in utter disbelief.

"Fuck…" He breathed. "What the hell was that?"

"You tell me." I leaned back against the wall. "One minute, I was dancing and the next minute, you were sticking your tongue down my throat.

"My tongue was nowhere near your throat," he said, now smiling. "And you left out the next minute where you were kissing me back."

"No, no, no. I was simply reacting to a sudden and rude intrusion of my mouth…" I paused, shaking my head. "You know what? I think I definitely had way too much to drink tonight, so I'm…I'm going to go lay down…Can I use your room?"

He readjusted my dress and smoothed my hair before answering. "Sure."

I expected him to walk away and leave me to get there on my own, but he grabbed my hand and led me down the hallway—past the bathroom and past the door that separated his suite from the rest of the place.

He unlocked the door to his room and hit the lights, motioning for me to get into his bed.

"Wait…" I felt a sudden chill hit my skin, bringing attention to my still slightly damp dress. "I need to take a shower…Can I use your shower for a few minutes?"

"Of course you can," he said, his eyes locked on mine. "You know you never have to ask me for anything like that…"

We stared at each other, and I was pretty sure that dampness I was feeling was not my dress.

"Um…" I stepped forward, looking away from him. "I'm going to go um…Take that shower now…" I moved past him and walked straight into the bathroom, but I saw his reflection in the mirror behind me seconds later.

He took a towel from the closet and handed it to me. "Here."

"Thank you…" I said, wondering why he was shutting the door. Shutting the door without leaving…

"You're not going to stay in here with me the whole time are you?"

He smiled. "Why wouldn't I?"

"Do you watch Josh when *he* takes his showers? Do you get off on watching your friends naked?"

"No," he said, smiling wider, looking me up and down and making my heart race all over again. "I was only going to help you get undressed because you're not completely sober yet, just in case you can't do it yourself."

"I'm pretty sober, so I think I'll be perfectly fine." I felt my cheeks heating. "I take off my own clothes every day, all alone. So, I think I can manage…"

"I'm just being a good friend, Ari."

"Yes. A *friend*, Carter."

"A *good* friend."

"Yes…" I was definitely more than drawn to him right now. "You've said that already…"

Our eyes locked again and I felt like I couldn't even force myself to look away.

"Okay. I'll wait in my room until you're done." His eyes lingered on my lips for a few seconds, and then he left.

Swallowing hard, I shut my eyes and tried to think.

This is a dream, Arizona. A very sexy, titillating, yet random as hell dream…You did not kiss Carter. He did not kiss you. You

*like him as your friend and you do not find him that attractive.
You're in his bathroom because you probably just went to the beach
together and wanted to freshen up afterwards...Yes...Yes... That
makes much more sense*

I opened my eyes again and turned on the water—holding my
hand underneath the faucet until I felt like it was warm enough. I
pulled the shower lever forward to turn on the overhead streams.

Then I realized I hadn't taken off my clothes yet.

That I *couldn't* take off my clothes.

The zipper on the back of my dress was jammed, and I now
remembered Nicole forcing it up a bit before we came to the party.

I considered ripping the dress off myself, but the fabric was
too thick, so I decided against it. I walked over to the door and
called Carter's name.

He walked down the hall to me seconds later, with a knowing
smile on his face. "Yes, Ari?"

"Could you please help me take off my dress?"

"Just your dress?" He raised his eyebrow.

"Yes." I stepped back inside, letting him follow me. "Just. My.
Dress."

"Okay. Turn around."

I turned around and felt his hands in my hair, felt him slowly
pulling my hair on top of my head and attempting a makeshift bun.

He gripped my zipper and jerked it a few times before it gave,
and then he slowly pulled it down until it reached my lower back.

I started to turn around, started to thank him, but he gripped
my hips and held me still. Gently tracing the line above the clasp of
my bra, he looped his fingers underneath the clasp and tore it free.

"Do you need help getting out of anything else?" he whispered.

I shook my head, completely turned on.

With my back still to his front, he hooked his fingers under
the straps of my dress and pushed them down my shoulders—
pushing the fabric down my arms, down my waist, down my legs.

He pressed his mouth against the back of my neck as he took off my bra, and then he whispered into my ear. "Are you sure you don't need help with these?" He tugged at my panties.

"I'm sure…"

"Okay." He kissed the back of my neck again and left the room.

I was pretty sure I stood there for twenty minutes, not moving, not blinking, and only trying to figure out what the hell that was.

When I finally came to my senses, I stepped inside the shower and stood directly under the streams. Shaking my head again and again, I kept wondering if it was a dream. Wondering why I was reacting so strongly to him all of a sudden.

He's like a brother to me…I shouldn't be thinking about him like this at all…

When my skin was red and raw, I turned off the water and stepped out, noticing he'd placed a white robe across the vanity for me.

I dried off and put it on, heading back to the bedroom so I could go and pass out.

Carter looked up from his desk as soon as I entered the room. "Ready to go to bed?"

"Yes, but um…You're not…" My heart still hadn't returned to its normal rhythm. "You're not going to join me, are you?"

"No…" A slow smile spread across his lips as he stood up. "Not unless you want me to."

"Are you implying sex right now?"

"Are *you*?"

My eyes widened, and he laughed.

He picked me up and tossed me onto the bed, fluffing the pillows and pulling the covers over me. He pulled out a few bottles of water from his mini fridge and set them on the nightstand next to me.

"I'll come back and check on you in the morning," he said. "Do you need anything else?"

"Um..."

"Um?" He raised his eyebrow. "You're starting to say that word a lot..."

"I..." I felt a sudden oncoming of sleep. "I think you're sexy as fuck, and if you weren't my best friend, and this wasn't a dream, I'd totally fuck you right now... "

"Excuse me?"

Everything went black.

track 9. tell me why (3:13)

Carter

What the hell was that?

I couldn't get the last thing Arizona said out of my mind, nor could I stop picturing the way her mouth and body felt against mine at the party yesterday. That meant a lot considering the fact that I was pissed about two major things right now...

Sighing, I wiped the last of Tina's vomit out of my car and clicked the text she'd just sent me: "I didn't know I was so drunk... Sorry I messed up your car...I was serious about wanting to do anal sex first though...Call me when you see this!"

Ugh. I put my phone back in my pocket, returning back to thoughts of last night.

The second I'd seen Arizona in that red dress, I couldn't focus on anything else. Not even Tina, and I'd tried. Hard.

I'd done my best to seem interested in Tina's bland and over-sexed conversation, to act intrigued when she not-so-subtly showed me the color of the thong she was wearing, but no matter how many times she whispered how badly she wanted to ride me later, I could only think about Arizona and how badly I wanted to be with her.

What's more, was when the two of us danced together at the end of the night, it didn't feel as playful and innocent as it normally did. And I knew she could feel the difference, too; she'd never blushed around me before, and she definitely never touched me the way she did either.

I'd checked on her a few times after she'd gone to sleep in my room and when I noticed that she'd rolled off the bed and onto the floor, I made her wake up. I held a wet towel over her head as she quietly cursed at me, made her drink a bottle of water with aspirin, and then I waited until she fell asleep again. I was honestly beyond tempted to spend the rest of the night with her to make sure she remained okay, but Tina had found me and was begging me to take her home so we could have sex.

Maybe her vomiting all over my car was a good thing...

Still thinking, I walked down my driveway and unlocked the door to my backyard—coming face to face with the second reason I was pissed.

Red cups and beer bottles were everywhere, and quite a few people had passed out on the Slip N Slide's yellow tarp. The Jell-O pool was overturned, white T-shirts were hanging from a makeshift clothing line, and there were numerous partiers who'd made pillows out of some of my appliances.

I headed inside, looking for Josh so I could kill him.

"Hey, what's up?" He smiled as I walked into the kitchen, holding up a frying pan.

"Do you see all those red cups and beer bottles in my yard?" I looked around my house. "On the floor in here, too?"

"Don't worry about any that," he said. "Last semester's newest class will be over in an hour to clean up everything. You want eggs?"

"No." I grabbed an orange juice from the fridge. "Will the furniture be put back today as well?"

"Yep." He flipped his eggs over. "Everything should be put back in order no later than three o'clock today...Maybe after you see how well everything is put back together, we can set up another business meeting about hosting an 'Epic: Part Two' party?"

I gave him a blank stare, and he laughed.

"I'm kidding, I'm kidding. I saw you leaving the party with Tina around three. How did that go?"

"It didn't," I said. "She vomited in my car as soon as we hit the highway."

"Oh. Well, let me guess. You helped her clean up and stuff when you got to her place?"

"Of course I did." I rolled my eyes. "I'm not as big of an asshole as you. How was your night?"

"Eh. I've had way better pussy, but it was still good."

"Do I even want to know who the unlucky victim was?"

"No, not unless you promise you won't judge me."

"I will." I laughed and stepped back. "Whatever extra stuff you put in the Jell-O shots this time, you should seriously reconsider that next time you want to throw an 'epic' party."

"Epic with a capital E, my friend." He smiled. "And why would I reconsider anything? Because one person got sick?"

"Because everyone got sick." I waved around the room. "Or do you not notice the twenty extra roommates we have this morning?"

"Noted. If you change your mind about another party, don't forget that I'll be willing to show you my worthiness around three today."

I didn't bother responding. I walked down the hallway and into my room, noticing that Ari was struggling to sit up.

"Stop." I placed a pillow behind her back and helped her.

"Thanks..." She looked up at me. "Can I ask you something?"

"Ask away."

"Did we really kiss each other last night or was that a nightmare?"

"Yes, we really kissed each other last night," I said. "But even if we hadn't, it would be more of a *wet dream* for you, not a nightmare."

"Forget I ever asked…" She tried to roll over, but I held her still.

"Do you remember any of what happened last night?"

"What do you mean *any of what happened*?" She looked terrified. "We did more than just kiss?"

"No…" I said, not sure how to feel about her not remembering. "Do you want to stay here for the rest of the day, or do you want me to take you home?"

"I honestly can't feel my legs right now…" She croaked as she pushed her phone toward me. "Can you text Chris and ask him if we can skip tonight and go out tomorrow? I'm too hungover…"

"Being hungover means you're incapable of *texting*?"

"I've texted your girlfriends before, and I didn't complain…" She narrowed her eyes at me, handing me her phone.

I tapped her message box and noticed that Chris had sent her a shit ton of messages since last night. "Are you sure this guy isn't the male version of Emily? He's texted you damn near every hour on the hour since yesterday. You should probably read his messages first."

She scooted to the edge of the bed, smiling and looking up at me. "Read them for me."

"You owe me a hungover Saturday at your place, with *breakfast.* "

"Done deal."

I clicked the first one. "'Can't wait to see you again, baby…' You've known each other less than two weeks and he's already calling you baby?"

"Just read them, without your unwanted commentary. Thanks."

I rolled my eyes and clicked the next one. "You're hot as shit, babe."

She smiled.

"You're beautiful as shit, babe."

She smiled again.

"I can't wait to see your—" I stopped. "I'm not reading the rest of this shit, Ari."

"Please…"

I groaned. "I can't wait to see your perfect ass tits and your warm ass mouth wrapped around my rock-hard cock…Can't wait to devour your pussy…"

Blushing, she snatched the phone away from me. "I didn't realize there were sext messages…Those are *private*."

"That's the type of shit that turns you on, Ari? Private message about warm ass mouths wrapped around rock-hard cocks?"

"It's called dirty talk."

"It's called an *attempt* at dirty talk…That's not what that is at all."

"It's exactly what it is." She narrowed her eyes at me, looking just as beautiful as she had last night. "Maybe if you'd done it with someone out of your plethora of girlfriends, your relationships would've lasted a whole lot longer."

I stared at her, noticing how she was biting her lip, how I was definitely going to have to find a way to stay the hell away from her for a while until I figured out why she was suddenly affecting me.

"Are you just going to stare at me?" she asked. "No smart ass rebuttals? No comeback puns?"

"No…"

"Well, that's shocking." She bit her lip again, and to prevent myself from pulling her up and biting it too, I grabbed a towel from the edge of the bed. "I'm going to take a shower. I'll talk to you when you're not talking about warm ass mouths and cocks…"

track 10. the best day (3:55)

Arizona

I remembered everything about last night. Every. Goddamn. Thing.

The way his lips felt against mine, the way he looked at me at the party, the way he rendered me utterly speechless when he undressed me in the bathroom. I'd never been kissed the way he kissed me, never felt it in every vein of my being and been left yearning for more. Much more.

Still, a part of me wanted to remain in denial, so I'd done my best to keep thoughts of him at bay today.

I looked at myself in a full length mirror, debating whether I should wear my hair up or down. My rescheduled date with Chris was tonight and regardless of the fact that I could still feel Carter's lips on mine, I needed to get back to reality. The one where we were just friends and had a shared drunken moment.

My phone buzzed as I decided to go with an up-do. Carter.

"Has your pussy been devoured yet?"

Laughing, I pulled my hair into a bun before texting back: "Not yet…Give it a couple of hours."

"A couple of hours for him to start or a couple of hours for him to finish?"

"Both….I'm sure he'll be down there a very long time. Something tells me you know nothing about giving and are all about receiving."

"Something tells me that you don't know me as well as you should."

Before I could even begin to comprehend what he meant by that, he sent me another text: "Have fun on your date tonight. Let me know how it goes later."

"Thanks…I will."

He sent me a colorful picture of a skeleton lying in bed with the words "I'll be waiting" and I laughed, now realizing that despite the amazing kiss we'd shared, and the outlandish sexual text he'd just sent, it didn't mean anything to either of us. We were just friends.

Just friends…Just friends…

I put on another coat of pink lipstick, and heard a soft knock on my door. "Yes?"

"Arizona?" My roommate, Heather, knocked once more.

"Yeah?"

"You got a minute?"

"Sure, come in." I leaned close to the mirror and plucked an errant hair from my eyebrow.

She stepped inside, smiling at me through the glass and I smiled back. When I'd first moved off campus and into our shared house, I'd thought that she and the rest of the girls would become some of my closest friends, but that never came to be. They were all majoring in medical studies, and since their schedules were practically the same, they tended to keep to themselves for the most part. With the exception of our early morning conversations around the coffee maker on the weekends, we always saw each other in passing.

"Me and the girls of the house wanted to give you this," she said, handing me a pink gift box. "It's a farewell present since you're the only one who's not staying in town after the summer."

"But I'm not going anywhere for another two months…"

"Yeah, but everyone is always all over the place now that we're working our residencies, and we can never all be here at the same time, so I didn't want to forget." She pulled a tiny blue box from her back pocket. "This one is for Carter."

"Why does Carter get a gift? He's not a roommate."

"No, but we see him just as much as we see you." She shrugged. "My boyfriend is downstairs now. I just wanted to give you that before we start watching our movie."

"Thank you." I was truly flattered. "I really appreciate this."

"You're welcome." She gave me a quick hug and left as quickly as she had come in.

I untied the box's bow and started to unwrap the gift, but Chris called me as I was tearing the first flap.

"Hello?" I answered.

"Are you ready or do you still need a little time?"

"I'm ready."

"In that case, I'm at your door."

"Be right down." I grabbed my clutch and headed downstairs, checking myself in the hallway mirror one last time.

I opened the door and saw Chris standing there with a huge bouquet of yellow flowers.

"You look beautiful…" He pulled me close for a kiss, gently slipping his tongue against mine and whispering against my mouth; I only felt a small tingle. Nothing groundbreaking.

Slipping his arm around my waist, he led me to his car and held the door open—smiling as I slipped inside.

"I never took you for a guy who likes pop music," I said as he turned on the radio.

"I don't…I just remembered that you do, and that I'm supposed to do whatever's necessary to get you to sleep with me later."

I laughed at his dry humor and hummed along to the music as he drove. Tonight was in fact our third date, and even though he was joking, I knew the three-date-sex rule was playing in his mind.

We pulled up to the pier half an hour later and walked hand in hand to Emilia's, an Italian restaurant that everyone at the beach loved. Since he'd made a reservation, we were immediately seated near the window, and the waiter came over with a complimentary house wine and asked to take our orders.

As he was writing down what I wanted, I spotted Carter sitting at a corner table. With Tina. He was dressed in a white shirt that was unbuttoned at the top with black slacks, and she was wearing a dark green dress that left little to the imagination.

Although Carter looked somewhat detached, he was holding her hand on top of the table.

I took out my phone and shot him a quick text. "You decided to try the relationship thing with Tina instead of just sex? When did that happen?"

"It didn't. What would ever make you think that?"

"The fact that you're holding hands at Emilia's and she's wearing a dress that looks like she wants to give you the ride of your life later tonight…"

"You really need to get better at sexting…" He tossed back a shot as he looked around the room until he found me. His lips slightly parted as his eyes met mine, and it looked like was about to get up and walk over, but he stayed back and texted me instead. "She called and said she wanted to go out to dinner   I didn't have anything else to do so I agreed…And if her dress says she wants to give me the ride of her life tonight, what the hell does yours say?"

"It says, 'I know you want me right here, right now…'"

"More like, 'I want to be fucked right here, right now…'"

I laughed and looked up to see him smiling at me.

"What's so funny?" Chris asked.

"Nothing, just a text from a friend." I put my phone away and gave him my attention. "Thank you for being nice enough to reschedule our date for tonight."

"Nice enough? It wasn't that big of a deal. I would've waited until next week if you wanted." He picked up my hand and held it. "Don't take this the crazy way or anything, but I really like you. There's something about you I can't quite put my finger on, but I like you a lot."

"Is this the part where you're going to tell me that I complete you?"

"It is." He laughed, letting my hand go. "How did you know?"

"Instincts." I sipped my wine and the two of us steered the conversation toward the simple and safe things: Plans after college, the bullshit of grad school programs, and the dwindling days of summer.

When the waiter returned to refill our wine a second time, I pressed a napkin against my mouth. "Will you excuse me for a minute, Chris? I need to go to the restroom."

"Of course."

I stood and made my way to the back, looking over my shoulder at Carter and Tina who seemed to be engrossed in a deep conversation. Regardless of what he'd texted me, I knew he was going to sleep with her, and I couldn't believe I was feeling slightly jealous; that was something I'd never felt when it came to him and whom he dated.

Sighing, I walked into the restroom and reapplied my lipstick. I added a bit more mascara and blush, and hoped that Chris had something else up his sleeve for our date tonight before he asked about sex.

I made sure I didn't leave anything on the sink and stepped out into the hallway, noticing Carter heading in my direction.

"Are you following me?" I crossed my arms.

"Unless you're coming from the men's restroom, I don't think so."

An elderly couple walked between us, and he grabbed my hand—pulling me toward a set of windows.

"Is your date not going well?" he asked. "Do you need me to call your phone and fake an emergency for you?"

"What? No...I actually need for you to leave. You're distracting me..."

"Come again?"

"You knew I was coming here on my date, Carter." I said. "We have an unwritten rule."

"And what unwritten rule is that?"

"That everyone who knows us, or everyone who has ever been around us, thinks we're screwing each other when we're not, so the less time we spend at the same places when we're dating other people, the better."

"First of all, I'm not *dating* Tina. Second of all, *she* picked this restaurant. You never actually told me where your date was going to be tonight..." He raised his eyebrow, looking concerned. "What is going on with you? Did you drink too much alcohol today, too?"

"Maybe." I sighed, silently counting the four glasses I'd just had with my dinner. "I just...I just thought you were here because...."

"Because *what*?"

"It's nothing." I took a deep breath. "I'm very sorry. I thought you were purposely showing up here to distract me."

"And why would I ever do something like that?" He looked completely confused.

"You wouldn't; hence the apology I just gave you." I started to move around him, but he stepped in front of me, gently pushing me against the wall.

"Are you sleeping with him tonight?" he asked. "Does he live up to everything on your spreadsheet?"

"I don't have a spreadsheet anymore," I said. "I'll have to find the time to start a new one because after the 'Epic' party, *someone* found a way to delete it from my phone."

"Hmmm. That's such a shame...."

"It is." I laughed. "I also hope that whoever that person is, knows that I could possibly charge them with a crime because even though it was just a cell phone, logging into someone's personal data cloud is—" I didn't get a chance to finish my sentence. My intended last word ended on his lips once his mouth covered mine and he kissed me again—taking complete control, making me feel everything I felt at that party all over again.

"Carter..." I panted, slowly pulling away. "What are you... What are you doing?"

"Now I'm *purposely* distracting you." He looked into my eyes. "I'm also trying to determine whether or not I'd feel the same thing if I kissed you while I was completely sober."

"So, what's the verdict on that?"

"Jury's still out." He walked away from me without another word, and returned to his table—leaving me completely speechless.

I leaned against the wall for several minutes, struggling to compose myself. I waited until the butterflies in my stomach stopped fluttering, until my heart stopped beating abnormally, and took a few deep breaths before returning to my table.

"You okay?" Chris asked as I took my seat. "I was about to come looking for you."

"I'm more than fine." I smiled. "You ordered us five different samples of wine?"

"Yeah." He moved to my side of the table and put his arm around my shoulder. "I want us to try them all together You ready to focus?"

"Absolutely..."

I tried, but I honestly couldn't focus for the rest of dinner. No matter how many times Chris gave me a compliment or told me a joke I'd normally find hilarious, my mind wandered back to Carter, back to both of us kissing each other senselessly at that party. To him kissing me again in that hallway.

When the restaurant manager informed us that he'd be closing the place early tonight, we left the restaurant and headed to Sandy Park.

Chris found a spot that was secluded by overgrown trees and turned off his car. He looked over at me, possibly gauging my reaction and I smiled.

With that he climbed into the backseat and pulled me back there with him.

We didn't waste any time talking.

His lips latched onto mine, and I desperately wanted to feel that reckless and uncontrollable passion—that raging desire that I'd felt for Carter just hours ago, but there was nothing. It felt like we were just going through the motions.

Not noticing my lack of enthusiasm, he slowly pulled away from my mouth, and started to kiss his way down my stomach.

Maybe this part will be good… This part will make me forget

I leaned back against the seat, and he hiked up my dress. He pushed my panties to the side and kissed the inner skin of my thigh. Caressing my legs, he whispered, "Nom, nom, nom…nom, nom nom…"

What the hell did he just say?!

"Nom, nom, nom…"

Oh my god…

"I love eating pussy…I'm going to eat yours all night."

I was pretty sure my vagina dried up like a desert and cried at that very moment, so I sat up before it could attempt to detach itself from my body and walk away for good. "Wait, Chris…I'm…"

"Not ready yet?"

NEVER… "Yeah…It's still kind of soon…I'm just not ready."

"I figured," he said, sitting up. "You've seemed a bit off since we left the restaurant."

"I'm not off...I just..." I figured I could still blame it on the alcohol. "I shouldn't have had so much wine—especially coming off one of the worst hangovers I've ever had yesterday."

"Ah." He nodded. "I've been there..." He helped me back into the front seat. "Well, I'll take you back home so you can get some rest."

"Thank you very much..."

Our drive home was slightly awkward. We didn't say much to one another outside of commenting on how annoyed we were with the usual summer migration of tourists, and when we arrived at my house, he was still a perfect gentleman. He opened the car door for me and walked me to the door.

"Try Sprite and fresh lemons," he said.

"For what?"

"Your upcoming hangover tomorrow morning." He kissed me and walked back to his car, motioning for me to go inside so he could pull off.

As soon as he shut the door, I slipped out of my shoes and dropped my purse to the floor. I heard my roommate and her boyfriend laughing in the living room, so I dashed into the kitchen and grabbed a bottle of wine and a mug. Then I went upstairs and shut myself inside my room.

I poured the first cup, slowly sipping it as I thought about the past forty eight hours. I could see everything playing in my head like a movie, and I kept pressing pause on my favorite frames, wondering if after all this time I could possibly like Carter after all.

He gave me wedgies on the playground in fourth grade...

I poured another cup, drinking it faster than the first.

He set my science project on fire after I told him he was ugly...

Shaking my head, I got into bed—fresh cup of wine in hand and leaned back against my pillows, thinking about everything as thoroughly as possible.

As I replayed our kiss from the party in my mind, I felt my phone vibrating. Him.

"How was your date?"

I hesitated before responding. "AMAZING! I had the Best. Sex. Ever!"

"I asked how your "date" was…not your daydream…"

"How was YOUR date? (Why is it so hard to believe that Chris and I had sex?)"

"It wasn't a date. It was just a dinner. (Because I know you didn't.) What are you up to right now?"

"I'm drinking cheap wine out of a mug."

"Want some late-night Chinese to go with it?"

I looked at my clock and realized it was long past midnight. "Only if I get three eggrolls that I don't have to share…"

"Sure. Be there in twenty."

I got out of bed and straightened my room, something I never did when he was on his way over. I moved my food and beverage magazines to the window sill and cleared my desk of all my half written recipes, leaving only my notebook so it would like I'd been writing.

I made the bed—tucking the sheets in for the first time in months, and as I was vacuuming, I suddenly stopped.

What the hell am I doing?!

I returned the vacuum to the closet and finally changed out of my dress. I put on the most unflattering pair of sweats I owned— along with a large T-shirt, and pulled my hair into a low pony-tail. To perfect my "look like a bum" effort, I found my makeup remover wipes and brushed them against my face until every bit of foundation and mascara was gone.

When I finished, Carter walked into my bedroom—Chinese food in hand.

"I lied about the eggrolls," he said, setting a brown bag on my desk. "You're going to have to share at least one of them."

"That wasn't part of the deal."

"It also wasn't part of the combo special." He tossed me a fork and froze—looking around my room with his eyebrow raised. "Did you and Chris come back here after your date?"

"No…What makes you think that?"

"Because this is the cleanest I've *ever* seen your room." He handed me a white box. "Is your mom coming to visit you tomorrow?"

"No…I just…I just felt like cleaning up."

"Right…" He took a seat on the edge of my bed. He stuck his fork in my bed of rice and lifted a piece of chicken onto his plate. "What really happened on your date? There's no way he brought you right home in that dress."

"We found a park and…" I paused. "Everything was going right for the most part but…"

"Do I even want to know the rest of this story?"

"No, but for future reference, if you ever start going down on a girl, please refrain from saying 'Nom-nom-nom'. It kind of kills the mood."

A smile spread across his face, and he held his laughter back for all of five seconds.

I rolled my eyes. "Feel free to stop any time now."

"I can't." He laughed harder. "That's really sad. So much for your 'pretty decent' sex."

"No, what's sad is a guy who claims he's going to sleep around for the summer, but he's not able to get it up for several days in a row." I leaned back against my pillows, laughing.

"Is it really that funny?"

"You not being able to have your infamous "rough and dirty" sex? Yes, it definitely is…" I shut my eyes, still laughing, and the next thing I felt was his lips on mine. Threading his fingers through my hair, he kissed me harder, rougher—forcing me to open my eyes and look at him.

There was no sudden break away, no "what the hell was that?" between us. There was only a shared look of understanding, a silent confirmation that I wanted him to take things further. *A lot* further.

Pulling away from my mouth, he trailed his fingers against my lips. "Is there any reason why you decided to put on the worst clothes you own before I came over tonight?"

"What makes you think I would do something like that?"

He didn't answer. He slowly slipped a finger into my mouth, and groaned when I flicked my tongue against it. Smiling, he slipped in another finger. "You can't lie to me, Ari..." he said, pushing his fingers in and out. "I see right through you."

"These aren't my worst clothes...", she muttered around his fingers.

"They are." He smirked, moving his fingers away. "But they're not going to prevent me from fucking you tonight..." He pulled me out of the bed and made me stand in front of him.

He ran his hands across my breast—palming them through the fabric of my shirt, making me moan as he gently twisted my nipples. "Take off your clothes..."

I stood still, entranced by the feel of his hands on me.

"Ari..." He squeezed my breasts.

"Yes?"

"Take off your clothes."

I hesitated for a few seconds, and he leaned forward and gently bit my bottom lip.

"Right now," he said.

I grabbed the hem of my shirt, but he placed his hands over mine and helped me pull it over my head. Without him saying anything else, he pulled the drawstring on my sweats, keeping his eyes on me as he stepped back and took off his shirt.

My breathing slowed as he unbuckled his jeans, as he slowly stepped out of his briefs and exposed his cock.

Oh my god...

I could feel my jaw dropping, feel redness crossing my cheeks, but I somehow managed to get out of my panties without taking my eyes off of him.

He grabbed my hand and placed it against his chest—trailing it across his abs, then lower and lower until I could hear his breathing slow with every touch.

His mouth latched onto mine again and his hands went around my waist, gripping me so tightly I could feel his fingers digging into my skin. Sliding his hand down a little lower, he slapped my ass. Hard.

"Ahhh…" I cried out as he did it again. And again…

The sharp pain was a complete contrast to the softer way he was kissing me, and I couldn't explain why, but I loved the way he was making me feel.

I moaned as he began to slow our kiss, as he suddenly pulled away from my mouth and spun me around. His cock was against my ass, and his mouth was on my neck—softly biting my skin.

Shutting my eyes, I felt him running his hands up and down my sides, heard him whispering, "Am I allowed to fuck you the way I want to?" He bit me a little harder. "Or do you have a spreadsheet for that, too?"

I shook my head.

"Yes to fucking you the way I want to…" He slid a hand between my thighs. "Or yes to the spreadsheet?"

"The…" I stuttered as he pressed his thumb against my swollen clit and rubbed it. "The first one."

"Good." He suddenly bent me over my desk—pressing my chest against cold metal, and spread my legs.

I heard him unwrapping a condom behind me, heard him saying, "You're so wet " as he trailed a finger against my slit.

Gripping my hips, he leaned against me and pressed kisses against my spine.

One kiss. Two. Three…

I tried to focus on the warmth of his mouth, the strength of his hands, and when I was finally picking up on the pattern of his kisses, he started to slide inside of me.

Slow at first, very slow...

He forced himself deeper and finally filled me, and then he placed one last kiss on my back before pulling back and pounding into me so fast and hard I nearly lost my balance.

"Fuck, Ari..." He rasped. "You feel so good..."

"Ahhh...Ahhh..." I murmured as he reached between my legs and strummed my clit, never stopping his reckless rhythm—thrusting in and out of me again and again.

"Carter, I...." I could feel my legs trembling, feel my pussy throbbing. "Carter, I..."

"Shhh..." He pulled out of me and flipped me over, grabbing my legs and wrapping them around his waist before sliding into me again. He looked into my eyes, pressing his fingers against my mouth as I moaned.

Unable to hold on for too much longer, I tightened my legs around his waist, and when he thrust into me again I lost all control. I started to cry out his name as I reached my climax, but he covered his mouth with mine—muffling me as he reached his own release.

Panting and trembling, I shut my eyes—not answering any of his questions that he peppered with forehead kisses.

The next thing I felt was him pulling out of me and lifting me up, placing me into my bed. I heard him step out into the hallway bathroom and run water, and then I felt him wiping a warm cloth between my legs.

He placed another kiss against my forehead, whispering, "I love the way you say my name when you come..."

With my heart still racing a mile a minute, I had no idea what the hell I should say to that. No idea how the hell Chinese food had turned to fucking...

I just continued to lay in bed with him beside me, with him running his fingers through my hair and softly caressing my neck.

I was certain he had nothing else to say either, because hours later, he fell asleep and I was still staring at my pale white ceiling. I tried shutting my eyes and forcing sleep, but my body wouldn't allow it.

My lips wanted to be kissed again, my thighs wanted to be caressed, and there was a yearning ache between my thighs that I'd never felt before.

To make sure I wasn't dreaming, or stuck in the middle of one of my recent fantasies, I looked over at Carter and made sure he was asleep. Then I trailed my hand down between my thighs—touching to see if my clit was in fact really swollen or if I really was—

"You're still horny?" Carter whispered, a smile in his voice.

I ignored him and immediately moved my hand away, keeping my eyes glued to the ceiling.

"Ari?" he asked again.

I didn't answer.

He let out a low laugh and moved on top of me, looking into my eyes. "*Ari…*"

"Yes?"

"Are you still wet?"

"No."

Smirking, he slid a hand between my thighs, getting the true answer to his question. "Would you like me to help you with this?"

I shook my head and he leaned down, sucking one of my nipples into his mouth. "Why not?"

I couldn't answer. He was circling his thumb around my clit and sucking my nipple even harder.

"Should I take your silence as a yes?" He slipped a finger inside of me and I barely managed a nod.

His eyes met mine and he smiled, not asking anything else.

He took a pillow from his side of the bed and positioned it underneath my lower thigh. Pressing his lips against my forehead first, he slowly kissed his way down my body—teasingly darting his tongue against every inch of my skin.

When he made it to my stomach, he spread my legs apart and blew warmer kisses against me. Then he suddenly pulled me forward and buried his face into my pussy.

My hands immediately grabbed his head, trying to push him away, to fight it, but he paid me no attention. He sucked my clit into his mouth—flicking his tongue against it repeatedly.

In utter bliss, I writhed against his mouth, and he held me still—not letting me get away.

"Carter…" I murmured. "Carter…"

He didn't answer. He released my swollen clit from his lips and slipped two fingers in and out of me—pushing them deeper each time I said his name.

"Come on my face, Ari…" he whispered and I leaned back against the pillows—shutting my eyes and letting another orgasm rip through my body.

I kept my eyes shut until I could feel my legs again.

When I finally did open them, I saw Carter looking at me with an "Are you okay?" expression on his face.

I nodded and a slight smile crossed his face. He got another washcloth and wiped between my legs. Then he stared at me for several minutes, not saying anything for a while.

"I'll be right back," he finally spoke, disappearing into my bathroom.

I heard the water turn on, heard him brushing his teeth, and I rolled over before he came back.

Fully sated, I smiled—still in utter disbelief about 1) How good that fucking felt and 2) That I'd just slept with my best friend.

"Goodnight, Ari," Carter whispered into my ear, rolling me over to face him.

Or, so I thought.

He rolled me on top of him and then to the other side of the bed. "You hate sleeping on the right side, remember?" he whispered, and then, with one arm wrapped around my waist, he told me to go to sleep.

It was much easier that time…

track 11. i knew you were trouble (1:55)

Carter

Shit...

tenth grade

Carter

Subject: Basketball tryouts.

I think I'm going to try out for the practice squad next week. If I get selected, they say I won't be eligible to play varsity until my junior year. You think I'll make the cut?

Sincerely,

Carter

Subject: Re: Basketball tryouts.

Yeah. From what I recall, you're pretty good, although I think your ego is already big enough. Do you really need any more attention from the girls at our school? … You may also have to explain those two tattoos you have on your arm when you get your uniform. (Still can't believe your mom took you, a minor, to get them…)

Wait a minute…Isn't the reading of your dad's will today? (It's rude to email during stuff like that…)

Hoping you're okay,

Arizona

Subject: Re: Re: Basketball tryouts.

I already told the coach I have tattoos. He said that if I'm any good, most people won't care, and that I wouldn't be the first high school basketball player to have tattoos. (I still can't believe that she acknowledges she's a "mom.")

My dad's will reading is over. (It's rude to leave your only son and cheat on your wife...)

I'm more than okay.

Sincerely,

Carter

Subject: Re: Re: Re: Basketball tryouts.

Where are you?

Still hoping you're okay,

Arizona

Subject: Re: Re: Re: Re: Basketball Tryouts

In my room.

I told you I was okay already. (Trust me.)

Sincerely,

Carter

I put my phone on silent and leaned back on my bed, staring up at the ceiling.

Today had been one of the worst days of my life, so I was lining up things to make tomorrow better: I was going to have sex after school with my girlfriend if she wasn't still upset with me for not telling her why I hadn't been to school for the past three days. (I refused to talk about my family with anyone.) I was also going to go back to my favorite sketchy tattoo parlor and get another tattoo on the inside of my arm—some type of tree so I could add onto it for years to come. Then, I'd probably need to spend some time with Arizona at the end of the day. Being around her always made things better for some reason.

I grabbed my white earbuds from the nightstand and placed them into my ears, shutting my eyes and drifting to sleep.

Or, so I thought.

Just as my favorite album began to play, one of the earbuds was ripped from my ear, and a blur of pink and purple crawled over me and took over the left side of my bed.

Arizona.

"What the hell are you doing?" I narrowed my eyes at her. "Did my mom let you in?"

"You really think that?" She dangled a silver bracelet in front of my face. "I told you I made a copy of your house key in shop class months ago. Your mom is passed out on the couch…"

"Of course she is…" I said. "Well, I need to be alone so I can think. So, no offense, but I don't really want your goddamn company right now, and since you had to literally break into my house to even see me, I'm going to ask you to leave."

"Okay." She stared at me, blinking. Then she put my left earbud into her ear and reclined against my pillows.

"Did you hear what I said, Arizona? Do I need to repeat it?"

"I heard you perfectly," she said, motioning for me to lie back down next to her. "You said you were going to ask me to leave because you don't want my company. So, when you actually *ask me to leave*, I will…"

Her eyes met mine and I knew she could tell that I was far from okay, that I was an emotional wreck today, and that I did really want her to stay.

Instead of fighting the facts, I lay next to her and put the other earbud in my right ear. "You being here today and seeing me like this didn't happen."

"It never does…"

track 12. the moment i knew (4:09)

Carter

I stood in Arizona's kitchen the morning after we'd had sex, brewing a fresh cup of coffee. Two of her roommates, Jenny and Heather, were standing across from me—waiting for the timer to sound.

"You know you can technically get coffee as it's brewing right?" I asked, noticing that they were staring at my chest.

"I'm aware." Jenny blushed. "Just waiting like you are…"

"I actually did not know that…" Heather stepped forward and held her mug under the coffee machine. "Learn something new every day. Just in case I don't see her today, will you tell Arizona to pick up some dish soap when she wakes up? It's her turn."

"I will." I nodded.

The timer went off and Jenny stepped forward, deliberately rubbing her mug against my chest before holding it under the coffee machine. "Sorry. Couldn't help myself." She laughed.

"Anyway," Heather said, ignoring Jenny. "In addition to the dish soap, could you also tell her to get us some more coffee? It's her turn for that, too."

"Noted." I noticed Jenny was still touching me. "Don't you need to get to work?"

She blushed again and stepped back. "Whenever you want me to leave my boyfriend for you, just say the word. *Say the word...*"

"I won't." I laughed.

"You will." She sipped her coffee and headed toward the door, laughing back. "I'll be awaiting that phone call!"

I waited for them to leave, made sure the car had revved up and pulled out of the driveway before I sat down.

My mind immediately attempted to process what the hell had happened last night in a series of frames: Movie. Laughter. Uninterrupted Kiss. Sex. Sex with Arizona. Sex again with Arizona. Sex with my best friend for as long as I could fucking remember, Arizona...

"Morning." She walked into the kitchen wearing a plush white robe, avoiding my eyes.

"Morning."

"Did you or one of my roommates make the coffee?"

"I did."

"So, there's no hazelnut?"

"No." I stood up and made her a cup, adding the hazelnut shots that I always left out whenever I made the coffee. While I was adding her usual three packets of artificial sweetener, she took a seat on the barstool across from me, still avoiding my gaze.

"What do you have planned for this weekend?" I slid her mug across the counter.

"My usual summer weekend routine: Gayle's with you at some point, stealing a class from the culinary school and hoping I won't get kicked out. Oh, and late night drinks with Nicole on Sunday."

"If she doesn't stand you up."

"Yes. If she doesn't stand me up." She took a long sip of her coffee—finally letting her eyes meet mine. "What about you?"

"Gayle's with you at some point…I have some errands I need to run and I need to pick up a few books on the law school's summer reading list. I'll probably do something with Josh as well."

Silence.

She brought her mug to her lips and tilted it higher, nearly downing the entire cup.

"Your roommates want you to know that they need you to buy more coffee and dish soap," I said. "They claim it's your turn so whenever you get a chance—"

"We're really not going to talk about last night?" She cut me off. "We're just going to act like that shit didn't happen?"

"No." I smiled. "What part do you want to talk about, Ari?"

"How about the part where my best friend since fourth grade *fucked me*? Or maybe we should discuss the part where he took my silence and utter shock to mean that I wanted him to perform cunnilingus on me? Yeah, you know what? Let's start *there*. Shall we?"

"First of all, I've been your best friend since *fifth grade*. I hated you in fourth grade, and we didn't start speaking cordially until the end of the year. Long after you got me in trouble for like the fiftieth time."

"Out of all the things I just said, *that's* what you want to discuss first?"

"No." I walked over to her and placed my hands on her shoulders. "So, we had sex last night. It happened, and from what I recall, you weren't very 'silent' about anything…"

Her jaw dropped and I laughed, shutting her lips with my fingers.

"I'm kidding," I said. "I don't think we have to have an intervention-type discussion about it, though. Last night doesn't change anything between us."

"You promise?"

"I do."

"Do you also promise to never talk about it, or let it happen again because we don't want to lose each other as friends, and we both know that sex ruins friendships? Undeniably and inevitably *ruins* them?"

"Is that a question or a statement?"

"It's both…"

"In that case, yes." I cupped her face in my hands and looked into her eyes. "We won't let it happen again because we both value our friendship too much."

"Good…" She exhaled. "So, just to be clear, last night never happened."

"Correct." I tucked a strand of hair behind her ear and stepped back. "I was never here."

"Great." She slid off the barstool. "Well, I'm going to get ready for a class and then I guess I'll see you tomorrow at Gayle's Can you pick me up around eleven thirty?"

"I can."

We stared at each other in silence, not saying anything else.

"Okay, well…" She stepped back. "It's only nine so…You go home, I'll stay here, and, um…I'll see you tomorrow?"

I averted my gaze away from her lips. "Sounds about right."

"Oh, and Carter?" She looked at me.

"Yeah?"

"It was definitely fourth grade. We became best friends in *fourth grade.*"

"You need to let that go." I laughed and headed for the door. "It was definitely fifth."

———

I couldn't make the shower water hot enough. I needed it to tear at my skin harder, faster. Regardless of what I'd said to Arizona at her place, it was going to take a hell of a lot for me to forget last night for a number of reasons: One, it was hands down the best sex I'd ever had in my life. Two: Her soft pleas and moans were still playing through my mind on repeat. And three: I'd actually felt something while we were looking into each other's eyes at one point, something that had never happened to me during sex before.

Shit...

Frustrated by the water, I turned it off and stepped out of the shower. I wrapped a towel around my waist and walked into my kitchen.

"Long night?" Josh set his newspaper down and looked up at me.

"Not really. Just stayed over at Ari's."

"Let me guess, she made you watch another one of those boring ass cooking shows and 'allowed' you to sleep on her couch?"

"Pretty much."

"Ridiculous." He stood up and followed me over to the fridge. "I need you to explain something important to me."

"I thought you'd never ask," I said. "It's very true what your last ex-girlfriend said: You really can't dress for shit."

"Forget you, man." He laughed. "I want to know how you continue to do it."

"How I continue to do *what*?"

"How are you still 'just friends' with a girl?"

"Do you realize that you and I have this same exact conversation every six months?"

"I know, and I'm not knocking you and Arizona. I know you two are strictly platonic, I'm just wondering about this in general. Like, how do you never consider crossing the line?" He leaned back against the counter. "I'm only asking because since we'll both be going to law school in the fall, and I think that's what I need to pick up—a girl who's just a friend."

"They don't sell friends in stores..."

"Come on, tell me. How do you *do* it?"

A memory from last night, one of Ari whispering my name as she came against my mouth suddenly crossed my mind. "You just go in having that in mind, and you should probably learn how to be a friend to her, too. Don't make things sexual like you tend to do."

"Right…Well, what if the girl looks like Ari, though? How does someone like me, someone with balls—unlike you, not act upon that?"

Ari's face post-orgasm crossed my mind again. "You just… Don't. I guess."

"Okay, okay, okay." He tapped the counter. "You. Me. The Bakery Bar. Tonight. Instead of a one night stand, we're going to find me a platonic friend. The uglier, the better."

"I'm honestly ashamed to call you my friend sometimes."

"The feeling is mutual, buddy." He grabbed a bottle of water and returned to the couch.

When I was sure he was deeply engrossed in his reading again, I poured myself an early shot of vodka and tossed it back. I was definitely going to need to be buzzed to keep my mind off Ari's lips for the next few hours…

Or days.

Or…shit.

Again…

track 13. the last time (4:56)

Arizona

The sex was a mistake...Just a one-time mistake...
I repeated those words all morning long until I halfway believed them, until I made my way into the class I was currently stealing: Pastry Design.

I took an apron off the rack and found a seat in the back, waiting to see if there would be a no-show today so I would have a station to use, but to my surprise, there was one with my name on it.

In utter disbelief, I slowly stepped forward—running my fingers across the lettering to make sure it was real. Then I noticed that there was a note next to my name, so I opened it and read:

> *How ironic is it that the best person in the class isn't really in the class at all?*
> *This is only for the summer...*
> —*Chef Brandt*
>
> *PS—I want to talk to you about some other culinary programs that may be good for your future career...*

I looked up and saw him nodding at me from the front of the room, a quick sign of approval.

Grateful, I took today's assignment card out of the pocket, hoping it would be something intricate enough that would keep my mind off of Carter.

Today's assignment:
You are to make a soufflé using only the ingredients in your fridge.
Today's theme is "Unrelenting Passion: Just One Night."

I dropped the card to the ground.

———

Hours later, after my "professor" made me fill out a few applications for four of the top culinary programs in the world, I found myself walking along the shore barefoot—letting the warm winds knock at me left and right.

No matter how badly I'd tried to think about something else today, anything else, Carter's rough touches, kisses, and caresses kept coming to mind. I guessed the dirty sex part about him was true, but a part of me couldn't help but want to believe that last night was about a little something more than just sex.

No, stop it…Just sex…Just friends…

I pulled out my phone and called Nicole.

"Hey there!" She answered on the first ring. "How are you today?"

"Good. How are you?"

"Great! I'm really looking forward to tomorrow night. I'm going to drop off some drinks and snacks at your place on my way to work tomorrow, so we can drink before and after the club. I even got us some DVDs."

"You were serious about having a slumber party after we go out?"

"Totally. I am determined to make Josh's party up to you."

"It's not that big of a deal, I swear. The thought is appreciated, though."

"Stop being so nice about telling me I'm a terrible friend." There was a smile in her voice. "I'll be over around eight, okay?"

"Okay…"

"Wait a minute. Why do you sound like that?"

"Like what?"

"Like…Like you're sad or depressed or something. Are you okay?"

I slept with Carter…Say it…I. Slept. With. Carter.

I couldn't get the words to come out. I wanted to tell her, but a part of me—a very strong part, was telling me to hold back.

"Arizona?" she asked. "Arizona, are you there?"

"I'm here. Nothing's wrong. I just had a long day in culinary class."

"Bummer. I forgot about that…Have you seen Carter today?"

"Yeah, earlier. Why?"

"Well, I know you're going to think I'm crazy, but do you think you could tell him I'm interested and just see what he says?"

"Um…"

"Um yes, or um no?"

Um hell no. "Sure. I'll tell him that the next time we talk."

"Well, in that case I guess I'll have an answer within twenty four hours!" She laughed. "Oh! Just got a customer. I'll see you tomorrow at eight!"

"See you tomorrow at—" The phone beeped before I could finish my sentence.

I dipped my toes into the ocean a few minutes before deciding to take a trolley straight to Gayle's. I figured one of their waffles would make me feel ten times better right about now, and maybe even help me think about this situation a little more.

Especially since Carter won't be there…

No, Carter *was* there.

As soon as I stepped inside, I spotted him sitting in the back. I debated whether or not I should leave and just wave down one of their mobile trucks, but he suddenly looked up at me.

I could literally feel myself being pulled toward him, as if I wasn't in control of my own functions. I took one step, I took two, and before I knew it, I was sitting in front of him.

Neither of us said a word.

"I put in your order as soon as I saw you walk through the door!" Our regular waitress walked over with a tray.

"A Belgian waffle with vanilla yogurt and strawberries—with a sprinkle of chocolate chips." She smiled at me as she set down my usual. "And a waffle tower with chocolate yogurt, peanut butter, and a sprinkle of Oreo chips and gummy bears on the side for you." She set a plate in front of Carter. "Could you two do me a huge favor and mix it up every now and then? Don't you get tired of ordering the exact same thing every time?"

"Could I have an extra waffle today?" Carter smiled. "For *free*? Will that help?"

"You're lucky I actually like you, kid." She laughed. "I'll bring it out after I get my next two tables." She winked at us before walking away.

"So…." I said, stopping. My first question was always what he did the night before, but I already knew the answer to the question. *Me.*

Seemingly picking up on that, he intervened. "Has Nicole sent you her usual, 'I can't hang out with you this weekend, but I'll definitely make it up to you' text yet?"

"Not yet. I think she's going to follow through this time. She said she's going to buy me lightweight-safe drinks all night tomorrow, and then she wants to hang out at my place afterwards."

"You believe her?"

"I do." I nodded. "The only thing that shocked me text message wise today was Chris. He asked if we could meet up again this weekend…"

"I think he really likes you. Are you going to give him a chance and maybe just have sex since that's all it was supposed to be anyway?"

"No." I picked up my fork. "I don't think I'm capable of having casual sex like you are."

He raised his eyebrow.

"I mean…His strange sex sounds aside, all we had was attraction and sweet kisses, but I need more than that to form a connection. Even if it is only for temporary sex. Besides, it's not worth starting anything anyway since I'll be leaving eventually, you know?"

"Not necessarily. Long distance relationships can work under certain circumstances."

"What circumstances?"

"None." He laughed. "I was just trying to give you a false sense of hope."

I smiled and cut my waffle, and for the next hour it was as if things were absolutely normal between us. I was actually convinced that us having sex last night wasn't going to change us at all.

When it was time for the bill, Carter covered it as usual and boxed up my leftovers. Unlike usual, he pressed his hand against the small of my back when we stood up, and he left it there until we got to his car—sending my nerves into a frenzy with a simple touch.

We didn't talk on the way to my house, and I noticed that he'd neglected to turn on the radio. The only noise between us was the wind and rushing traffic.

Two stoplights from my block, he finally spoke. "After all these months of stealing classes from the culinary school, they still don't care that you've never paid a dime of tuition?"

"Shockingly, no. It hit me a few weeks ago that they only call security on me when it's exam day, and the professors really like me. My passion, anyway. Did I tell you that one of them wrote me a recommendation letter for a few other schools?"

"No." He laughed as he pulled over to the curb. "Please tell me that you actually read it and made sure he didn't say that you're a thief anywhere inside."

"He did not!" I laughed with him, opening my door. "He said I was brilliant and possessed some of the most fervent passion he'd seen in years…He did mention my "creative means" to learn, but there's no way they'll equate that to me stealing classes."

"Let's hope not."

"Thanks for the ride." I shut the door. "I'll hit you up tomorrow if Nicole bails on me."

"She will."

"She won't!" I quickly walked away and rushed inside my house.

I put my hand over my heart and exhaled; it was racing all over again.

This was so not good…

track 14. speak now (3:42)

Arizona

I slept late the next day. All day.

I even called in sick to my part time job at the marina and let my manager berate me for the umpteenth time. (Something about if I was ever late again or called in sick one more day I would be fired. I didn't care about the fired part, it was more about losing my boat access pass that I sometimes needed to use when the chefs held classes on Parker Island; private boat fares weren't cheap.)

When I'd finally found the motivation to drag myself up, it was six o'clock and I figured I should start getting ready for a night with Nicole. I went downstairs to see what she'd dropped off earlier and found myself standing in a sea of plastic bags—bags full of all types of junk food: Cheetos, chocolate bars, twenty different types of fruity candy, and lots of vodka and beer.

It was just like Nicole to literally drop something off without thinking about putting it away. By the time I finished stuffing everything into the pantry, it was seven o'clock and she'd sent me a text:

"Soooo don't kill me for this, but I have to cancel on you tonight! I have a really, really good reason though! It has an eight pack and I'll tell you all about it tomorrow, I promise!"

WHAT THE HELL?

Holding back a frustrated scream, I typed a text: "This is the tenth-plus time you've stood me up for a fucking guy, Nicole. A non-boyfriend guy at that and I'm beyond tired of it! You have no idea what it means to be a good friend, so the second you decide that you want to be one, let me know." My finger hovered over the send button, but I didn't press it.

She wasn't worth it anymore.

I grabbed some of the snacks she'd bought and headed upstairs to my room.

I flipped through a few cooking channels and settled on a chef that was making a specialty crème brûlée. I changed into a different set of pajamas and got into bed, grabbing my binder to take notes.

As the chef was testing the custard's temperature, my phone vibrated. Carter.

My mind immediately pictured him kissing my lips and holding my body taut against him, so I knew I didn't need to talk to him right now.

I hit ignore.

He called again.

I hit ignore again.

He sent me a text: "Are you hitting ignore because you don't want to admit that I was right about Nicole?"

"You were wrong about her actually. We're at my place taking shots and eating pizza. I'll call you later."

"I'm looking at her right now, so unless you've grown a beard and a mustache within the past six hours, I take it that she did, in fact, bail on you?"

"Unfortunately...The guy she's with has a beard and a mustache?"

"Yes. He also looks like he's at least ten to twelve years older than her."

"You're kidding."

"Not at all. What are you really doing?"

"Moping about what pitiful friends I have. (You included.) You?"

"Getting ready to head home. I was trying to help Josh find a "just friend" friend at the bar tonight."

"Did it work?"

"No. He decided to go for the one night stand option instead. You want some company?"

"Not really…" I lied.

"Well, I do. Be ready in twenty. I'll pick you up and we'll come to my place."

"What's wrong with my place?"

"I would answer that, but it never happened…"

I blushed. "Okay. See you in twenty." I didn't bother changing out of my pajamas. I put on a pair of old worn sneakers and took a duffle bag out of my closet.

I walked downstairs and stuffed most of the things Nicole had bought inside of the bag.

"You going to a slumber party, Ari?" Heather looked up at me from the counter, smiling. "Aren't we a little too old for those?"

"No, Nicole stood me up again so I'm going to hang out with Carter for a while."

"Oh. Well, sorry to hear that about Nicole, *again*. At least Carter was free tonight, right?"

"Right." I paused. "I slept with him the other night."

"You slept with who?" She tilted her head to the side.

"Carter. I slept with *him*. We had sex."

"Right…" She put her hand over her chest and laughed loudly. "Like I'd ever believe that! You two are like the cutest non-couple/best friends ever." She looked down at her work again. "Have fun."

"I'll try " I slung the duffel bag over my shoulder and stepped onto the porch. I was certain that most people wouldn't believe we'd had sex either; hell, even though I had the memory to prove it, a part of me was still in disbelief.

Carter pulled up just as I was sitting down. Instead of waiting on me to make a move for the car, he walked up the pathway and reached for the duffle bag.

"Are you planning on asking me to move in?" He held it up. "What the hell is in this?"

"Snacks and alcohol, courtesy of Nicole."

"Well, at least something good came out of her standing you up this time." He slipped his hand around my waist—sending those familiar, palpable tremors down my spine, as we walked to his car.

We made the short drive to his place without saying much of anything to each other and like always, I adjusted his music from indie rock to soft pop.

I wanted to say something, to laugh and joke about something insignificant, but all I could think about was how badly I wanted to feel his lips on mine again.

"Arizona?" His voice broke me out of my thoughts and I realized he was holding my door open. "Are you going to get out of the car? Why do you always stare into space when the car is parked?"

"Bad habit." I got out and followed him inside. As we walked down the hallway, we could hear soft moans and groans coming from Josh's bedroom.

I tried my best to tune them out as Carter led me into his room and shut the door.

"Are you actually going to talk to Nicole about flaking on you this time, or are you just going to let it go like you normally do?" he asked, setting the duffle bag on the floor.

"Honestly? I think I'm just going to stop agreeing to go out with her...She'll get the point eventually, and maybe then, when she realizes what's happened, we can talk."

"Makes sense." He popped open a drink and handed it to me. "Were you two really planning on watching any of these movies?"

"Why?"

"Because they're all terrible..." He shuffled through the DVDs. "I know I'm the one who wanted company, but can we bypass the chick-flick thing?"

"In exchange for what?"

"I'll watch one of your cooking shows in exchange for any of these... *When Harry Met Sally*? *Maid in Manhattan*? *The Breakfast Club*?"

"*The Breakfast Club* isn't a chick flick." I snatched that DVD from him. "I doubt she and I were going to make it through any of these."

"Good." He picked up the remote and turned on the TV, flipping it to the cooking channel I was watching before.

The chef had moved on from crème brûlée and was now getting ready to prepare a seven course meal.

Carter handed me the remote and a handful of snacks. "Need anything else?"

"Would you like to take turns painting our nails when the show goes off?"

"Not at all. Is this a re-run?"

"Maybe. Why?"

"I'm just wondering," he said, getting in bed behind me. "I wanted to know if I would be able to talk to you during the show."

"You're the one who was lonely and needed company. I was just fine."

"Is that so?"

"Yep." I turned up the volume. "And even though it is a re-run, and you claim you hate cooking shows, I know deep down you love watching them with me."

He laughed, but he didn't say anything else. He pulled me back by my shoulders until I was leaning against his chest.

I swallowed, ignoring the sudden tension between us and kept my eyes glued to the TV.

"Make sure you have the oven preset to 375 degrees. Not 350, not 400. 375…" The chef took out another set of ingredients.

Carter blew a soft breath against my neck and my breathing slowed. I tried to ignore the fact that my heart was now racing, that I could literally feel myself getting wet.

"This is how you want to season the vegetables…" The chef was smiling at the camera, showing off his different brushes, but I wasn't paying any attention. I couldn't.

Carter was kissing my neck every few seconds—letting his teeth softly graze my skin, and my body was betraying me by reacting to his every move.

"Could you get us some ice from the kitchen?" I broke away from him once his hands began to massage my shoulders. "And some glasses, please?"

"Sure." He smiled and stood up, leaving the room.

Shaking my head, I took several deep breaths and tried not to think too much. Then I moved to the other side of the bed, at the end, by his dresser.

Carter returned to the room and looked at me, holding back a laugh as he set the ice on his desk. He filled one of the glasses with juice and walked over, handing it to me.

"Any reason why you moved down here?" he asked.

"The view is better from here. Much better."

"Do you mind if I join you and see for myself?"

"Yes." My cheeks were on fire. "Yes, I do mind…You seemed to enjoy the view from where you were on the bed before, so…" I stopped talking once I realized he was ignoring me and moving behind me anyway.

He pulled me against him again and began to run his fingers through my hair.

I tried to zone in on what the chef was saying again, but it was no use. I'd seen this episode hundreds of times, cooked the meal alongside him quite a few times, and I could probably recite his recipe and instructions by memory.

Feeling Carter tug at my hair again, I turned around to face him. "Why aren't you paying attention to the show?"

"Because I'd rather pay attention to something far more interesting."

"Something like my hair?" I smiled. "Interested in the type of conditioner I used today?"

A smile formed on his lips and he looked like he was about to say something smart in return, but I beat him to it.

"Are you trying to have sex with me?" I asked.

"By running my fingers through your hair?" He smirked. "If that was the case, I think I would do something far more deliberate than that "

"Like attempting to kiss me?"

"*Attempting*?" He leaned forward and pressed his lips against mine. "No. I would just *kiss you* " He didn't let go of my mouth until I was breathless, and then he pulled me into his lap so I was straddling him.

Without saying another word, he ran his fingers through my hair, kissing my lips again and again.

"Do you…" I paused as he planted a kiss against my forehead. "Do you remember how I said we should forget how that night between us happened?" I asked.

"I have no idea what night you're talking about."

"You know exactly what I'm talking about."

"Is it in reference to when I 'fucked' you?" He smiled.

"Yes…" I pushed his shoulder. "Well…"

"Well?"

"Technically, we had sex in the early hours of the morning that day. It wasn't at night so…We still have the hours of today, which are included in the hours of the weekend, so…I think that we should have sex again but not past today. Because that way…"

"That way, *what*?" He pulled me close.

"That way we get to use the full weekend of um…sex, to our full advantage…And our friendship won't get messed up still because I think we can put this behind us when it's over…What do you say?"

"I didn't catch anything after you said, I think we should have sex."

I blinked and within seconds his mouth was on mine and my fingers were in his hair. He slipped his hands underneath my shirt and unclasped my bra, rubbing his hands up and down my back.

Slowly tearing his mouth away from mine, he whispered against my lips. "Are you still interested in hardcore?"

I blushed.

"Tell me…" He pulled my shirt over my head. "Do you still watch that?"

"Yes…"

"Good." He drew my bottom lip into his mouth and bit it gently. He placed my hands against his belt, silently commanding me to unbuckle it, and when I did, he lifted me out of his lap.

Taking off his shirt, he stared at me. "Take off your pants and get on the floor."

Hesitating, I stayed on the bed, instead watching him as he took off his own pants. My eyes veered to the bulge in his briefs, as he pulled them off, I swallowed.

"Ari…" He tilted my chin up with his fingertips. "Take off your pants…And get on the floor…*Now.*"

I didn't listen.

I leaned forward into his lap instead, pressing my lips against his cock.

He sucked in a breath as I took him into my mouth, threading his fingers through my hair as I bobbed up and down. His grip in my hair tightened and he tensed as I moved faster, as I felt him on the verge of coming, but he moved my head away.

Smiling, he gently pushed me out of his lap and ordered me to stand up.

Obliging, I stood in front of him and started to untie my pants, but he moved my hands away and loosened the drawstring himself. He leaned forward and pressed his mouth against my stomach—slowly trailing his tongue to the edge of my panties.

In one smooth motion, he ripped them off and pushed my pajama pants to the floor.

"Get on all fours…" he said, his voice low.

I looked at him a few seconds before obeying, letting my knees sink into his floor's plush carpet. I kept my eyes forward as he moved behind me, as I heard the sound of him unwrapping a condom.

His hands were on my sides seconds later, and he gripped me tightly. He slid one hand between my thighs and slid a finger against my wetness, sucking in a breath as I moaned at his touch.

Without warning, he thrust into me all at once—filling me completely.

I cried out and he pulled me back by my hair. "If you scream like that…" he whispered into my ear, "everyone in this house will hear me fucking you." He pounded into me again. "Is that what you want?"

I couldn't focus. He wasn't giving me a chance to respond.

"I thought you were the 'private' type, Ari…"

"Carter…" I moaned as he slid a hand up my waist and squeezed my breast. "Carter…"

"Yes?" He slapped my ass. Again and again.

I bit my lip to prevent myself from crying out, dug my nails into the carpet as I felt myself getting closer and closer to a release.

"Oh… Oh Oh god…". I felt him strumming my clit with his thumb. "Ahhh… Ahhh…"

Intense pressure was building between my thighs, and my legs were beginning to shake.

Out of nowhere, he stopped and held me still for a few seconds. His hands still firmly pressed into my skin, he whispered my name a few times before gently rocking into me.

Moaning, I felt him rubbing his hands against my sides—heard him saying, "Let go…"

He said my name one last time, and my body gave in at the same time as his; I collapsed onto the floor.

Pulling me back against him, Carter whispered a few things I couldn't understand before sliding out of me and tossing away the condom. He slid his hands underneath me and lifted me up, placing me into his bed.

I stared at him as he wiped between my legs and ran his hands across my breasts.

"Are you okay?" he asked, turning off the TV.

I just stared at him.

Leaning down to kiss my forehead, he climbed in bed next to me and wrapped his arms around my waist.

"What's wrong, Ari?" He looked concerned. "Was I too rough with you?"

"No…" I smiled. "I'm just not okay…I'm more than okay."

Smiling back, he kissed my lips, my cheeks, and my forehead again and again until I drifted to sleep.

track 15. everything has changed (3:43)

Arizona

The first time I woke up, I was laying on top of Carter. His hands were entwined with mine and my head was resting against his chest. Twice in the middle of the night, we'd woken up and had sex, and we'd somehow fallen asleep mid-kiss.

The second time I woke up, I was alone. And I was late.

The alarm clock was blaring loudly and my watch read 11:30. *Shit...*

I jumped out of bed—heading to my closet, quickly realizing that my closet wasn't here. Not in Carter's room.

I pulled his drawers open looking for something better to wear than flannel pajamas. I settled on one of his T-shirts and tied it at the back. I even tried on his pants—the smallest ones I could find, but it was no use. They fell off as soon as I buttoned them.

Shit. Shit. Shit...

I caught a glimpse of myself in the mirror and literally gasped. There were red marks all over my neck, my lips were puffy, and my hair looked like I'd spent one too many seconds with my fingers in a live electrical socket.

Not willing to risk being fired just yet, I pulled my hair into a messy high bun, licked my lips, and found a different shirt to cover up the marks.

The pajama pants would have to stay...

———

"Why are you wearing a turtleneck in the dead of summer?" My boss looked up at me as I approached the pier. "Have you forgotten what part of America you live in?"

"Not at all..." I said, sweating profusely. "I just felt like wearing a turtleneck today."

He looked at his watch. "You're lucky I actually need you today. Get in there."

I pushed the doors to the box office open and set down my bag.

My coworker Ashley looked up at me. "What's got you glowing today?" She smiled. "You and Scott finally made up?"

"No, we, uh, broke up actually. I'm not glowing."

"You *are*!" She stood up and walked over to me. "Tell me..."

Thankfully, I didn't have to change the subject or find a distraction on my own. A customer approached the window, and after we arranged her boat tour, twenty more customers drew near.

Per the usual summer season, the line became never-ending, the questions nonstop. By the time our lunch hour came around, flipping a coin for who should take a break first was far more important than discussing whether I was glowing or not.

"Heads it is!" Ashley clapped. "I'll be back in thirty minutes. You want anything?"

"No, thanks." I flipped our window sign to "Out for Lunch" and closed the blinds.

After she left, I began the less than thrilling task of counting the sales for the first half of the day. I was halfway through the children's tickets, when the fabric of Carter's turtleneck itched me to the point of no return.

I pulled out my phone and called him.

"Hello?" he answered.

"Can you do me a favor?"

"I've already forgotten about last night."

"That's not what I'm talking about...But I'm glad we're already on the same page with um   that. That thing which did not happen."

He laughed. "What's the favor, Ari?"

"Can you go to my house and get me some clothes and bring them to the marina?"

"Are you currently there naked?"

"No." I rolled my eyes. "There's a spare key under the flower pot on my front porch. Anything in my top right drawer—shorts, T-shirts, jeans, would be great. No tank tops, though. *Do not* get one of those."

"Why no tank tops?" There was a smile in his voice. "I'm pretty sure that'd be a perfect thing for you to wear today, unless you're trying to cover something up?"

Gasping, I hung up and returned to my spreadsheet. When I looked up again, I realized forty minutes had passed with no sign of Ashley, so I called her.

"Hey!" She answered on the first ring.

"Um hey..." I looked at my watch. "Um, do you plan on coming back before or after our shared hour is up? I would like a break, too, you know..."

"Oh! Time just completely passed me by! I'll be back in exactly fifteen minutes!"

"That'll only give me five for a break"

"Were you really going to walk around the boardwalk in a turtleneck, though?" She actually sounded genuine, like the act of stealing my break was doing me a favor.

"Could you at least bring me some lunch then?"

"I can try…" she said. "But you should've told me when I first asked you if you wanted anything back because now it's crowded out here, so—"

"Ugh!" I hung up. Moments like that made me question if working here for the boat pass was even worth it.

I browsed the menu of the pizza truck across from us and heard a knock at the door.

Maybe hanging up on her did some good, then. I thought. Maybe it made her come to her senses…

It didn't. It was Carter.

"Hey…" I said, letting him inside.

"Hey." He looked me up and down. "Interesting outfit." He set a white box on the counter and handed me my clothes.

I couldn't even get my mouth to say thank you right now. He was shirtless, dressed only in navy blue swim trunks that showed off his perfectly carved V and the small trail of hair that lined up with his zipper.

"Something wrong?" He took off his shades and I noticed that light beads of sweat were trickling down his chest.

"Nothing at all." I turned away and slipped inside the restroom, putting on the better clothes, grateful that the shirt covered all of his bite marks. I pulled out another shirt he packed and saw that he'd even packed me a brush and makeup.

Taking extra time to put myself together, I finally slipped out ten minutes later, only to find him sitting in my seat.

"I don't get a thank you?" He smiled.

"You don't get anything," I said. "If I could discuss the reason in question, you would know why…"

His blue eyes met mine and I shook my head, looking away from him. "What's in the box?"

"Lunch." He handed it to me. "I figured you probably didn't eat yet. Will I get a thank you for that, maybe?"

"Thank you," I said, flipping the lid open. It was a grilled chicken wrap and sea chips. "Ashley is stealing my break again..."

"I'm sorry to hear that."

"I bet...Where did you disappear to this morning?"

"Nowhere. I just went for a walk on the beach."

"Someone new you needed to break up with? How did she take it?"

"Funny." He let out a low laugh. "I just needed to think." He looked as if he wanted to say something else, but Ashley walked in.

"Well, hey there!" She exclaimed. "I rushed back so I could give you at least fifteen minutes of your break."

I rolled my eyes and glared at her. "How very thoughtful of you."

"I know." She sat down, batting her eyes at Carter. "I'll stay here while you go take your break..."

I grabbed my chicken wrap and headed toward the door, surprised that Carter followed me.

We walked toward the edge of the docks, not saying much of anything to each other. When I finished my wrap and noticed him staring at me, he smiled.

I awkwardly returned the smile and we spent a few minutes watching the seagulls fly above us.

"Thank you for bringing me clothes and lunch," I said, starting to head back.

"You're more than welcome. What are your plans after work?"

Avoiding you so I can think... "I'll be hanging out with a friend."

"Which friend?"

"You don't know her."

"I know all of your friends." He looked into my eyes. "Which one?"

I glanced at the cake box charm on my wrist. "Betty."

"*Betty?*"

"Are you having a hearing problem today?" I stepped in front of the box office door. "Yes. Betty."

"What's her last name?"

"Crocker. She's new to the beach, so I'm going to show her around after I get off."

"Okay, Ari." His lips curved into a sexy smirk. "Meet me at The Book Bar at six. Bring your friend Betty Crocker with you if she actually exists..."

———

At The Book Bar, neither of us spoke. The waitress must've assumed we were mad at each other, or not talking for a reason because she didn't bother greeting us. She simply set down two waters on our table and gave us her notepad and pen, letting us write down our own orders.

"So..." I managed, sipping my water.

"So?" Carter reached over the table and tilted my chin up with his fingertips. "So, what?"

"Nothing...Um...How was your night?"

"The same as yours, I believe." He smirked.

I looked away from him and blushed—quickly focusing my attention on my water again.

I definitely wasn't going to be able to look at him with a straight face today. I was hoping we could just get through this little rendezvous and I could go home and regain my sense of self in private.

I stuffed a few complimentary tortilla chips into my mouth and started to count the ones that were left. Then I noticed Carter getting up from his side of the table and sitting next to me.

"What time do you get out of your night class today?" he asked.

"It was actually cancelled..." My eyes met his. "I got an email from my teacher when we first got here."

"Anywhere else you need to go today?"

"No…" I swallowed. "But I don't want to go home yet. Unless you have something you have to do, that is."

He looked over at me and stared into my eyes for a while. "I don't."

"So…We should hang out."

"We should."

Silence hung in the air between us—so unfamiliar and strange, and the newfound attraction between us was electric, palpable. I wondered if either of us would start listing suggestions like we usually did, if those few rounds of sex had already ruined our ability to be just friends, because I was honestly unable to speak right now. My brain couldn't function properly when his lips were so close to mine.

"How about Marina Cove?" Carter finally shattered our silence. "Epsilon Chi is throwing a get-together there today."

"Sounds good."

"One of your beach bags is in my trunk. Do you need to go home and get anything else?"

I shook my head and he left a twenty on the table. Standing, he grabbed my hands and pulled me up, leading me to his car. He even opened the door for me.

I slipped inside and he cranked the engine—starting the one hour drive to a private cove that was near the shore. The waves lapping against each other to our left were the only sounds between us, and I tried to pretend like our hands weren't entwined behind the gear shift—like his fingers weren't caressing my knuckles at every stoplight.

As he veered the car onto the expressway, I put on my shades and stole glances of him every now and then. How the boy with itchy hair and gangly height from fourth grade had grown into the dominant and sexy man sitting next to me, I'd never know…

When we pulled up to the cove, our hands disentangled as we parked.

Several familiar faces from the EPIC party were setting up volleyball nets and grills, and Josh was yelling our names and walking over.

"Hey!" He looked surprised to see us. "You two decided to come after all, huh? Do you now have a change of heart about Epsilon Chi?"

"Hell no," we said in unison, laughing together.

"Then why are you here?" Josh crossed his arms.

"Looking for something to do," I said. "The beaches are cluttered with tourists and there's a big wedding at the pier, so we figured crashing your party and making you feel somewhat important would be a much better way to spend our day."

"Once again…" Josh said. "Out of all the girls in your elementary school, *this* is the one you chose to befriend?"

"You're just jealous it wasn't me and you," I said.

"I hate to break it to you, Ari," he said, "but it would've never been me and you because I would've hit it a long ass time ago."

"*Never.*" I opened Carter's trunk, taking out my beach bag. "I'm going to go change and lay out near the rocks. Whenever you guys start grilling, let me know and I'll help." I walked away and headed toward the restroom villa, hoping the brand new tension between me and Carter wasn't obvious.

I pulled my hair into a bun and found a perfect spot to rest. I lay against the rocks and took a short nap as the sun warmed my skin.

Josh called me over to help marinate some of the chicken just as I flipped over, and for once, we actually managed to be together for more than ten minutes without arguing.

With each hour that passed, more and more people pulled up to the marina—beach towels and beers in tow, and even though everyone was genuinely nice and friendly, the only thing I really wanted to do right now was lay against Carter again.

At sunset, a familiar hand grabbed mine and pulled me along the shore.

"Careful," I said, letting go of his hand. "People might actually think we've had sex."

"We *have* had sex."

"You know what I mean." I blushed. "They'll think we're together now, and I'm pretty sure we're not."

"We're still best friends, Ari."

"Best friends do *not* hold hands."

"I was only holding your hand to let you go," he said, looking amused. "We've walked along the shore and talked for hours far too many times to count."

"Yes, well…"

"Well, *what*?"

"Excuse me if I'm still adjusting to something that might've happened last night. Unlike you, I'm doing my best not to do little things that give you an inkling of an idea that it may happen again."

He suddenly stopped walking and stared at me. Then he pushed me into an oncoming wave.

My body hit the water and I laughed—swallowing salt water as another wave washed over me.

Standing up, I immediately ran toward him and chased him up and down the shoreline, trying to get him back.

I never did catch him, though. Whenever I got close, he would grab me by the waist and push me into another wave. Then he started chasing me.

Eventually surrendering, I held my hands up. "I'm going to take a break by the bonfire. I'm going to remember what you did, though."

"You won't." He smiled and I blushed for the umpteenth time today.

"Hey, Carter…" A brunette walked right between us. "And you're Arizona, right?" She acknowledged me without glancing my way.

I shot Carter an "I'll be over there" look and found a spot near the fire. I grabbed one of the vegetable skewers from the grill and watched as that girl fawned all over him.

To my surprise though, he wasn't giving her his usual charm routine. He was still smiling and entertaining her questions, but he wasn't giving her the full experience I'd come to know.

She said a few more things to him, things that looked like they were dripping with sexual innuendos, and then she walked away.

When she left, Carter walked up the bank and sat right next to me.

"Did you two set a date?" I asked. "When will you be going out with her?"

"I won't be," he said. "What made you ask me that?"

"It's your typical M.O. That, or taking her in the backseat of your car right after or—"

He pressed his finger against my lips. "I recently had sex with someone who might've ruined me for all others."

My eyes widened and my cheeks heated.

"Of course, it never actually happened in her mind, but I wouldn't be a good best friend if I lied and said the same…" He moved his finger away. "For the record, it's going to take me a lot longer to forget."

"So…This girl's pussy is magical?"

"Must be." He laughed.

"Do you think it's possible for this guy to have sex again with this best friend of his without the two of them fucking their friendship up?"

"I think it's very possible for them to have sex again, and I think he and this best friend can assess the damage afterwards "

"The woman in question is used to going on dates whenever she's sleeping with someone."

"Then the guy in question will take her on dates."

147

"But that's the problem," I said, feeling his hand subtly press against the side of my thigh. "Normal best friends don't go on dates."

"Then I'm starting to think we've never been normal…"

I hesitated a minute before responding. "Can we go back to your place tonight?"

eleventh grade

Carter

Subject: Some Advice for Your Date Tonight.
Please don't embarrass yourself by wearing a goddamn sweater.
Sincerely,
Carter

Subject: Re: Some Advice For Your Date Tonight.
Please don't embarrass yourself by talking for more than five seconds at a time.
So not sincerely,
Arizona

Subject: In All Seriousness...
Where is your date taking you? Do you have a curfew?
Sincerely,
Carter

Subject: Re: In All Seriousness...
Since he's a TRUE gentleman and not just into sex like someone unfortunate I know...He's taking me on a "whirlwind" date. (Every girl at school is talking about these

btw.) First, he's taking me to see a movie in the VIP section of Waldman's Theater. Then, we're going to Sandcastle to watch fireworks over ice cream...Then we're going to walk down the pier at sunset and get tattoos before a little star-gazing to end the night. (Take notes. THIS is how it's done.)

Where are you taking Monica? No, wait. Let me guess. Since she's already told you that she's looking forward to having sex and just wants to do something simple...

A movie and Burger King?

Get more creative,

Arizona

Subject: Re: Re: In All Seriousness...

A movie and McDonalds.

Sincerely,

Carter

As it turned out, Ari was more than right about that "whirlwind date" thing.

The second I picked up my date—Monica, who was ironically wearing a sweater, she'd said, "I'm so grateful you're not like other guys, Carter...I don't have to dress like a model to impress you and I'm sure you're not really taking me to a drive-in movie and a burger place like all the other guys I've been with..."

Of course not...

I googled "cheap whirlwind date," and pretended as if I'd planned to take her on one all along. I took her to a free art gallery and to Zapas—a restaurant a step above fast food fare. Then, because I was such a "nice guy," I took her to a private park.

When we returned to the parking lot, her true intentions began to surface. As soon as we got into my car, her arms went around my neck and her lips were against mine.

I reclined my seat and pulled her into my lap, rolling my windows all the way up.

She straddled me, kissing me harder as I ran my fingers through her hair. I slipped my hand underneath her sweater, running my fingers along the clasp of her bra. Before I could take things any further, my phone rang.

I ignored it, letting it continue to sound off in my pocket.

Monica moaned against my mouth, and my phone rang again, but I ignored it once more. Surely it was a misdial, and it couldn't have been anyone important; the people closest to me knew I was on a date.

Unsnapping Monica's bra, I palmed her breasts in my hands.

My phone rang louder, again and again.

Groaning, I gently lifted Monica out of my lap and placed her in the passenger seat. "Give me one second." I kissed her lips again before taking out the phone to see who it was.

Ari...

"This better be a goddamn national emergency..." I held the phone up to my ear.

"It is..." She was crying. Hard. "It fucking is..."

"Whoa. Hold up." I changed my tone. "What's going on? Why are you crying?"

"I'm sorry for calling instead of texting during your date, but..."

"But what?"

"After you take Monica home—whatever time that may be, could you please come get me?"

"Where are you?"

"Waldman Theater..."

"The one near the bookstore?"

"No..."she said. "The one by the airport..."

What? "Where is Elliott?"

"Gone...He left me here." She sniffled. "I'm perfectly fine... Just wanted to get a ride since the buses don't come out here. Oh, and before you ask, yes, I'll definitely give you gas money for driving all the way out here."

"I wasn't going to ask you for gas money."

"It was a joke…" She sniffled again. "Will you be able to get me?"

"Yeah."

"Thanks. See you later." She hung up, and I knew I wouldn't be able to give Monica my full attention right now, even if I tried.

I buckled my pants and cranked the engine. "Something important just came up. We'll have to finish this later…"

"Aww!" She blushed as she readjusted her bra. "You really are a gentleman! You want to wait until the second date until we have sex! I was *so* going to sleep with you today, but it's cute that you want to hold off for a bit!"

Fuckkkk, Ari…

I dropped Monica off in record time, with her promising a "more satisfying night" next weekend, and began the long drive to the airport area. I passed exit after exit, wondering what type of argument must have transpired between Ari and Elliott for him to leave her in the middle of nowhere.

Why the hell would anyone do that?

When I pulled up to the theater, Ari was sitting on a bench with a bucket of popcorn in her lap—looking at her phone. I pulled up to the curb and got out of the car.

"Hey…" I said.

"Hey…" She didn't look up as I sat next to her. "I hope you didn't cut your date short because of this."

"There were a few other reasons…"

"Oh?" She looked at me and I noticed that her eyes were red and puffy, that there were tears falling down her face.

"Yeah…" I untied the silk headband she was wearing and pressed it against her cheeks. "Turns out she wanted a whirlwind date, too. She also thought I was a complete gentleman, so she wore a sweater."

"Bahahaha!" She burst into laughter and I caught the popcorn bucket before it could fall to the concrete. "Oh god! I am...I am...Bahahahaha! That's what you get for trying to sleep with every girl possible."

"Glad my night of epic failure could make you laugh   " I waited for her to stop. "What happened to yours?"

"Turns out, you were right..."

"About?"

"Guys our age are really only interested in sex..." She paused, looking at me.

"Okay..." I said. "Are you going to tell me the rest of the story, or are you waiting for something?"

"I'm waiting for you to say what you're supposed to say. You know, that's not true, Ari. All guys our age aren't only interested in sex."

I blinked.

"Ugh " She shook her head. "He tried to put a move on me in the theater and I mean...I went along with it at first because he's a really good kisser. I mean a really, really good kisser. He does this thing with his tongue where he kind of—"

"Can we bypass all the flattery parts for the asshole who left you in the middle of nowhere, please?"

"Right..." She snapped out of it. "As we were kissing, he started slipping his hands under my dress and you know..."

"Fingering you?"

"Yes...Fingering me, and um..."

I raised my eyebrow, waiting for her to finish.

"It felt good, but awkward, you know? So, I asked him to stop and he did. We watched the rest of the movie and he just kissed me here or there. After the movie, we got into his car and I started to ask him if he wanted to get dinner since we had a few hours before the fireworks, but he started kissing and fingering me again and um..."

I pressed the scarf against her cheeks again.

"When I told him to stop this time, he got mad. He said he was tired of spending so much money on me without getting anything in return. He said he would only continue our date if I promised he would finally get to fuck me by the end of the night "

I sighed.

"So…I told him I couldn't promise him that, and he said he couldn't promise to finish our date either. Then he made me get out of his car and sped off, but not before saying, 'Thanks for wasting six months of my life…" Tears fell down her face again. "I should've believed you…I should've known."

"No, that's not it," I said. "He's just an asshole." I sent a quick text to my newest friend, Josh, regarding Elliot and tried to calm Ari down again. "I actually think it's kind of cool that you want to hold on to your virginity until you're ready."

"Really? You think so?"

"No." I couldn't keep a straight face with that lie. "But it's honorable. Lame as hell, but honorable."

"Have I mentioned that you're a dickhead this week already?"

"You just did." I smiled and pulled her up—walking her to my car.

"On the plus side, at least I'll get some sleep tonight and have energy to last through tomorrow's bake sale."

"Like hell you will." I cranked the engine. "I'm not letting a Saturday night go to waste, especially since I have blue balls already. We're both going to do something so this night won't be a complete bust." I veered onto the highway. "Where was lover-boy supposed to take you after the movie?"

"Sandcastle for fireworks."

"Ugh. And after that?"

"Gourmet ice cream."

"*Jesus*…And after that?"

"Tattoos."

"Okay, we can do all of that, but only if we get tattoos first. I'll need some pain to focus on to get through the rest of that shit."

"Deal," she said. "Now, tell me more about Monica's sweater. That was a joke, right?"

"I wish, my friend. I fucking wish…" I gave her the play by play of my night—every moment in detail, and by the time I was done we'd arrived at Hot Needle.

"Were you planning on getting 'Ari and Elliott forever'?" I looked over at her. "I hope you now know that would've been a terrible idea."

"I was going to get a key and a pen."

"Yes to the key. No to the pen."

"Okay, *Dad.*" She rolled her eyes. "What are you getting?"

"I don't know." I pulled a box of beer from underneath my seat. "Ask me after I've had four or five of these. You can have two."

"How very generous of you."

"I am, since you're a lightweight."

"If you drink all of those, I'm not letting you drive back." She took my keys and put them in her purse. "We'll call a cab to get home, and I'll take the bus with you tomorrow to get your car back."

"Deal," I said. "So, seeing as though we'll be able to see the fireworks from here, we can get your dreamy ice cream at a parlor after the tattoos. Wait a minute. I've never seen you eat any ice cream. I thought you only ate yogurt?"

"I do." She shrugged. "Elliot is the one who loves ice cream."

"Okay, forget that." I opened a beer. "Yogurt it is. I don't like ice cream that much either, you know."

"Unless you're after a girl who likes it?"

"Exactly. That changes my 'likes and non-likes' list instantly."

She laughed. "Why am I friends with you again?"

"Because no one else will put up with you."

An hour later, after we'd chugged nearly all of the beers, we stumbled into the tattoo parlor, trying our best to play sober.

Laughing at nothing at all, we happily handed them our fake IDs and design ideas.

She stuck to her key and pen, and I decided to let the designer have free reign on my right arm.

I didn't even realize what exactly he'd drawn until the next morning, when a snooty kid walked up to me on the bus and asked me why I had the State of Arizona on my arm...

track 16. love story (3:27)

Carter

"Hello?" Josh waved his hand in front of my face. "Hello?"

"What?"

"Are you going to be my wingman tonight or what?" He sipped his drink. "I get the blonde and you get the brunette." He pointed his head toward the girls in the booth across from us.

"Not interested," I said. "But I'll stick around for another hour or so."

"*Not interested*?" He looked dumbfounded. "Do you see the brunette? Do you see her body?"

I looked over again and she waved at me, blushing.

"I do see her," I said.

"So, what's the problem? Has your mission to get laid as much as possible this summer changed between last week and now?"

An image from last night, one of Ari straddling me in my car, crossed my mind. "Not really…"

"Good." He finished his beer and slammed the empty bottle onto the table. "Then be my wingman." He stood up and I followed suit, walking over to the other booth.

"Good evening, ladies." Josh signaled to the waiter as he sat down. "I'm Josh, and this is my good friend, Carter. Do you mind if we join you?"

They both agreed and I smiled my way through the first round of drinks and pointless topics, not paying any of them much attention. My mind was elsewhere, mainly on Arizona.

Ever since that day at the marina, we'd spent the last few nights at my place—watching her cooking shows and discussing random things like normal, but slipping in a brand new abnormal state of sex at the end of the night. Each and every time with her was more memorable than the last, and I'd never yearned to have someone so many times in a single night before.

Besides a few random messages she'd sent me this morning, we hadn't spoken much at all. She had an all-day cooking exam at the culinary school, and they'd told her that they wouldn't kick her out for a change.

Looking at my watch, I figured she should be home by now, so in the middle of the brunette telling me that she'd have her apartment all to herself tonight, I texted Ari.

"How did your test go?"

"I think I aced it." Her response was instant. "Really f-ing aced it."

"Good for you. Did you celebrate with your classmates yet?"

"Ha! You know everyone in the class hates me. LOL (I'm a "thief," remember?) I just came home and decided to bake myself an éclair."

"You only baked one?"

"Yes. Only ONE. :) What are you up to?"

"Out with Josh, role-playing wingman."

"Okay."

"Okay, *what*?"

"Nothing. How is it going?"

"You know you don't really care how it's going."

"If I didn't, I wouldn't have asked… How. Is. It. Going?"

"It's going so well that I'd rather leave and come to your house to celebrate your exam with you."

"Well, you can't."

"And why is that?"

"Because I don't want company right now, especially not from some guy I slept with last night, some guy who is now being a wingman so he can sleep with someone else!"

"Ari..."

"CARTER..."

"Does the all caps mean you're upset?"

"NO. NOT AT ALL."

I smiled. "In that case...First of all, I'm not "some guy," I'm your best friend. Second of all, did you not catch what I typed previously..."role-playing"? Pretty sure I would tell you if I was seriously looking for someone else...I always have, have I not?"

"..."

"If I can't celebrate with you in person, can you at least pick up when I call you after this? I'd like to have at least one intelligent conversation today."

"..."

"What does the "..." mean?"

"They mean yes."

"But no to me coming over tonight?"

"HELL NO to you coming over tonight. ☺"

"Carter?" Josh suddenly cleared his throat to get my attention. "Can I talk to you by the bar for a minute?"

"Sure." I followed him out of the booth and into a small hallway. "What do want to talk about?"

"Two things: One, tonight you've been a terrible wingman. Absolutely fucking terrible."

"I told you hours ago that I didn't feel like doing this tonight."

"Two..." He ignored my comment. "It's actually a good thing. Now that the brunette is convinced that you're as fun as a dead fish—"

"Her name is Farrah."

"Same thing." He shrugged. "They both want to come home with me...Just *me*." He stood there smiling, nodding his head slowly.

"Are you waiting for some applause?" I asked.

"No." He held back a laugh. "I just need you to hold off on coming home until later—a lot later. You know, so we can use the living room, and those floor to ceiling windows. I've always wanted to do something with those."

"Why can't I just go home first? Like, right now?"

"Because I just paid the check and they're more than ready to leave now." He gave me a pointed look. "*More* than ready."

"Whatever, Josh. Go."

"I knew you'd understand." He gave me a high five and returned to the booth.

A part of me was actually grateful that I wouldn't have to stay another second, but without being able to go straight home, I needed something to do.

Restless, I decided to drive around for a while, so I slid behind the wheel and hit the highway. When I veered onto a familiar exit, I pulled out my phone and called Arizona.

"Hello?" she answered on the first ring. "Is this Josh's wingman?"

"It isn't." I laughed. "Seeing as though he got both of the girls in the end, I don't think that's an appropriate title for me at all."

"He's going home with *two* girls?" She scoffed. "Are you sure he's the best option for a roommate for when the two of you start law school? You sure you don't want to find another one?"

"Not unless you plan on withdrawing from Cleveland and staying here to go to culinary school. I'd definitely pick you over Josh for a live-in roommate."

"Ummm." She was smiling; I could tell. "I very much appreciate the offer, but Cleveland is where I belong. How was your day?"

"Uneventful. Read a few early articles for the fall, fixed a few things on my car, and apparently made my best friend upset."

"Somewhat upset…She's not the psycho-jealous type."

"Hmmm." I suddenly didn't feel like driving anymore so I tried to find a parking spot. "What do I have to do to make it up to you?"

"You can give me a foot massage." She laughed. "That seems like something you wouldn't enjoy."

"I can do that," I said. "Open the door."

"*What*?"

"I'm outside your house. Open the door."

"What part of 'Hell no to you coming over tonight' didn't you understand?" There were papers rustling in the background.

"I must've misinterpreted that text…Open the door."

She hung up and the door opened seconds later.

"Yes?" Arizona narrowed her eyes at me, trying to look upset but failing at it. "Something I can help you with tonight, Carter James?"

"Letting me inside would be a good start." I stepped forward. "Or I can force you to if you'd like."

"I'd like to see you *try*…"

She stood there, not moving, so I picked her up—tossing her over my shoulder and made my way inside. I carried her over to the couch and tossed her onto it, and then I shut the door.

"You really only made one éclair to celebrate?" I asked.

"No." She grinned. "Yours is on the counter."

"Thank you." I walked over and picked it up—devouring it before joining her on the couch.

"That was very good," I said, smiling at her.

"Thank you…" She started to lean against me, as if I was going to wrap my arm around her shoulders, but I prevented her from doing that. Instead, I pulled her into my lap so she was facing me, so I could look into her eyes and taste her lips a few times.

"This doesn't seem like you're getting ready to prep for a foot massage," she whispered. "Do you know how those work?"

"I know exactly how they work."

"So why are your hands cupping my ass instead of my heels?"

"Because, while I will definitely be giving you a foot massage to make up for my completely minor offense tonight, I'm going to fuck you senseless first."

Her cheeks turned red.

"That is the point you were trying to get across when you sent me all those evasive texts before your exam this morning, correct?"

"Maybe…" She blushed again and I kissed her lips, slowly pushing her out of my lap.

"Bend over the couch…"

track 17. come in with the rain (5:12)

Arizona

I lay in bed on Friday night—anxious and unable to fall asleep. There was a light rain falling outside my window, and rounds of thunder were roaring in the distance.

My heart was begging me to text Carter, to ask what he was up to and if he wanted to come over, but my brain overruled it. Mostly because he'd just left my house a few hours ago.

God, I can't be this infatuated with him...

I rolled over and grabbed my headphones, thinking that maybe music would be all I needed to fall asleep, but then my phone vibrated. A text message from Carter.

"Hey. What are you up to?"

"Attempting to fall asleep. You?"

"Same. Would you like to go somewhere tonight?"

"Absolutely."

"I'll pick you up in twenty."

Practically jumping out of bed, I slipped into an old summer dress and flats. I pulled my hair into a low ponytail and decided to put on a little makeup. I brushed some shimmery pink eye-shadow over my eyelids and accented my eyes with mascara.

Just as I was putting on lipstick, Carter sent me a text—letting me know he was outside.

I looked myself over one last time and grabbed my purse before running downstairs.

"You're meeting me at the door now?" I stepped back once I opened it, shocked to see him standing there. "You normally wait in the car."

"You're putting on makeup now?" He smirked, lightly tracing the crease of my left eyelid with his fingertips. "You usually don't wear any if it's just me and you."

"I was already wearing makeup. I was trying a few different looks in the mirror."

"I thought you were attempting to go to sleep."

I blushed and looked away, caught in an easy lie.

He let up an umbrella and held it over my head. "You want to walk along the beach?"

"*No*," I said, dodging puddles as he led me to his car. "Even if it wasn't raining, hell no."

"Why not?"

"Because you and late night strolls on the beach never end well for the girl…"

"Fair enough." He laughed. "What about the movies?"

"We did that yesterday."

"Yes, but we didn't actually watch the movie. Maybe we can actually try to pay attention to it this time."

I fastened my seatbelt, now remembering how one second we'd been sharing popcorn in an empty theater, and the next he'd had me in his lap—saying his name until the credits rolled.

"No to the movies," I said. "I don't trust you. What's the best place you think you've ever taken one of your um…"

"Girlfriends?"

"Yeah." I realized we still weren't attempting to address what we were. "What about that nice grove where you took Sarah? Oh! And didn't you take Emily to that old train station? I remembered you telling me you loved that, so maybe there? Or, what about where you took—"

"Stop." He leaned over and pressed his finger against my lips. "You know how we've somehow adopted the unspoken rule that we're not telling anyone that we're having sex, how we're continuing to hang out with our other friends—pretending like we're not fucking each other recklessly every night?"

I nodded, unable to keep the redness on my cheeks from forming.

"Okay," he said, lowering his voice. "Well, even though I tell you everything—and I do mean everything, I have a new, unspoken rule of my own: the last thing I honestly want to do when I'm out with you is talk about what I did with someone else...So, whenever we're together from here on out, we're not going to talk about anyone outside of us. Okay?"

I blushed again. "Okay."

He drove out of my neighborhood and onto the main streets, holding my hand in his lap.

"What time does the docking section of the pier normally close?"

"Midnight, sometimes one o'clock if the employees feel like it."

As we approached a red-light, he looked over at me. "Well, since you work at the marina—"

"*Worked*." I cut him off. "I think I got fired today."

"What? How do you 'think' you got fired?"

"It was my turn to take a break first for a change and I took it I just never went back."

Laughing, he squeezed my hand. "Good for you. I was actually going to ask if you'd ever been on one of your company's boat tours."

"No " I said. "Ironic, huh?"

"Very, and I think we should fix that. Would you like to go on one?"

I nodded and he made a U-turn—speeding off into the night toward the other side of town. When we got there, we had to rush to the box office to buy tickets before they closed.

I silently thanked God that neither my manager nor Ashley were working tonight. Instead it was the tour guide himself, and since it was raining, he said we would be the only people aboard.

Undaunted by the small audience, he stated the trivia enthusiastically as the boat sailed across the dark Atlantic. He even gave us free drinks during the lags when there wasn't much to say, acknowledging that most of his jokes were terrible, but we laughed anyway.

Carter's arm went around my shoulder halfway through the tour and remained there for the rest of the ride. And every now and then, for no reason at all, he would tilt my chin up and kiss my lips for several minutes at a time.

"And now..." The tour guide said, as the captain steered the boat near a small island of lights. "This is Infinity Island. In the daytime, you'd normally be able to see people out and about and lounging on the sand, but since it's so dark..." He looked at his watch. "I usually pause the tour here and let the tourists get up and take pictures for about twenty minutes before the next stop so "

Carter and I exchanged confused glances.

"So, for my OCD purposes, I'm still going to have the captain stop here." He laughed. "Feel free to tour the boat and be back in twenty for the rest." He put down his mic and took out an e-reader, speaking into the small radio that was attached to his jacket. "Twenty minute stop, Barney. Three more stops and then we're done for the night." He held the reader up to his face and ignored us.

"Okay…" Carter took my hand and stood up. "Maybe you can give me a tour of the boat?"

"You'd probably know more than I do…I have no idea where anything is."

"They didn't teach you anything about the boat itself in your orientation?"

"They probably did…But I'm pretty sure I was reading a cooking magazine instead of the information manual that day."

Laughing, he pressed his hand against the small of my back, and we walked up to the top level where there was no covering. The rain was still falling—drizzling slightly, and we couldn't see anything in the distance.

I took out my phone and handed it to him. "Would you mind taking a picture of me? I want to remember this." I stepped in front of the railing.

"Night vision?"

"Yep." I smiled, holding it for the camera, but his finger didn't press the button. He was staring at me, looking confused. "Um…" I said. "Do I need to explain how a cell phone works? Have you forgotten?"

"No." He walked over to me and pulled me against his side. Then he held the camera above us. "Let me know when to press the button…I want to remember this, too."

"Oh…" I smiled. "On three. One…Two…Thr—"

He kissed my lips and snapped the photo at the same time.

"Is that good enough?" he asked, handing my phone back to me.

"No." I was still smiling. "I think I need a few more of those before we go back."

"Photos or kisses?"

"Both."

He pulled me close again and took three more, and then he led me toward the other side of the ship—where there was an antique style café. I thought he was going to open the door so we could take pictures inside, but he didn't.

Instead he grabbed my hands and held them above my head, pushing me against the door with his hips.

"We have ten minutes before we have to get back." He dipped his head to my neck and gently bit my skin. "Do you think they'll mind if we take a little longer?"

I murmured "No…" as he looked into my eyes, as he slowly hiked up my dress and made love to me against the door. Softly. Gently. Less reckless than before…

I screamed his name across the darkness, coming apart in his arms, and he took his time kissing me again and again until I felt like going back for the rest of the tour.

The boat had already started to move, and the tour guide didn't seem to mind how late we were when we rejoined him downstairs. By the way Carter pulled me into his lap and kissed me for the rest of it, I was sure that he knew what we'd been up to.

When we arrived back to the pier, we walked along the beach and talked for hours about absolutely nothing. I didn't want our conversation to end, but as the sun rose, I could feel myself getting tired, so he picked me up (tossed me over his shoulder) and took me home.

As if that date sealed it, the next few nights weren't even a question. He texted me and told me what time he was picking me up, and we went out together. Still uncomfortable showing affection in front of people we knew, we saved those moments for when we were alone, and our friends never knew anything different.

The things we normally did together felt new and exciting, no matter how hard we tried to pretend like they were the same. Those "you can take my bed, I'll sleep on the couch" courtesies were now completely invalid; even though we always ended up in each other's arms at some point in the night, we never discussed it in the morning.

I was pretty sure I loved him, and not in the way I loved him before.

This was different. This was "I needed to have him every hour of the day," "be around him whenever I could", and "do whatever I could to have him" type of way.

From the way he looked at me, I could tell he felt the same.

track 18. crazier (3:08)

Carter

Subject: OMG! GREAT NEWS!
Meet me at the pier at noon today. At that new sub place. I have something to show you.
Prepare your eyes!
Ari

Subject: Re: OMG! GREAT NEWS!
I'm pretty sure I've already seen it. Several times, last night, the night before, last week…
Sincerely, Carter

SUBJECT: Re: Re: OMG! GREAT NEWS!
This isn't related to sex, thank you very much.
Hurry up.
Ari.

An hour later, I spotted Ari in front of the sub shop, waiting for her to turn around and notice me. Her hair was pulled into a low ponytail, and her brown eyes were gleaming against the bright sunlight.

"Took you long enough." She looked me over. "I see you decided to actually wear a shirt today."

"Only because you told me this meeting wasn't related to sex." I almost pulled her into my arms for a kiss, but I held back. I still wasn't sure what the hell was happening between us, and even though we were more than intimate now, we had yet to show any public displays of affection; wasn't sure what that would mean if I initiated it.

"Do you want me to tell you the news out here or over lunch?" she asked.

"Over lunch." I motioned for her to follow me inside the sub shop and we took a seat in the back.

The waitress quickly took our orders, and promised to be back in less than ten minutes.

"So..." Ari said, smiling. "I actually have three sets of news, and I'm going to let you pick which one—"

"You look really fucking beautiful today." I cut her off, looking at her and wondering why I'd never seen just how stunning she was before. "Really fucking beautiful..."

She blushed. "Thank you..." She was silent for a while before speaking again. "You want the good news, the bad news, or the great news first?"

"Bad news."

"I ran into your ex, Emily, about half an hour ago and she yelled at me in front of everyone at the supermarket."

"What did she say?"

"That she hates me, she hates you, she hates your tiny little cock..."

"Is it *tiny* to you?"

Her cheeks reddened, but she ignored my question. "She said that if we ever end up together, that she will personally crash our wedding...With a personal army of cats, I'm sure."

I laughed. "What about the good news?"

"She tried to punch me and I took her down."

"Are you being serious?"

"Of course not." She scoffed. "Security took her down, but I did try." She smiled at the waitress as she set down our sandwiches.

"Do I even want the great news?"

"The *phenomenal* news, excuse me." She pulled a folded envelope from her pocket and slid it across the table. "Open it."

I set down my napkin and pulled out the paper—reading a brief letter from Collège Culinaire de France.

"They are deeply sorry for the enormous error in the processing of your previous application and would be delighted and honored to have you in their newest cohort of classically trained chefs," I read, genuinely happy for her.

"Read the rest..." She beamed. "That's not even the best part..."

I looked over it and summarized it aloud. "Since there was a mistake and this is short notice, based on your talent and recommendation letters, they're offering you a full scholarship if you confirm.

She practically squealed.

"Congratulations. I'm very happy for you." I started to hand the paper back to her until my eyes caught the bolded line at the bottom. "It says you'll need to arrive there June 16th, though. Is that right?"

She nodded, still smiling.

"That's *two weeks* from now, Ari."

"What?" Her smile slowly faded and she snatched her letter back. "No, it's not. It's..." She read the letter again and again. "I was reading it so fast when I got it this morning...I could've sworn it said July..."

"And it's an eighteen month program with no extended breaks?" I read more of the fine print. "You only get five approved holidays…The first approved holiday is in six months."

Her eyes met mine and neither of us said anything for a while.

I stood up and moved to her side of the booth. Her fingers effortlessly entwined with mine under the table, and I looked into her eyes.

"We'll make the most of it."

track 19. i'm only me when i'm with you (2:22)

Arizona

Two weeks might as well have been two seconds, and I was starting to wish that I hadn't emailed the French school with an all caps "YES" before meeting with Carter. I'd been so caught up in the moment, so elated that my dream of studying under the best was coming true, that I hadn't thought of what that would mean for us.

Whatever "us" was anyway…

We'd spent every waking moment together for the past several days. He helped me shop and get what I needed for the trip—even buying me a new suitcase and volunteering to ship whatever couldn't fit. We'd taken advantage of each other's bodies too many times to count, and most of our mornings were spent walking alongside the shore.

For years, I'd never understood what it meant when people said they felt like laughing and crying at the same time, until now.

———

I was standing in Margarita-ville, waiting on Carter to return with our drinks and I was trying to hide the fact that I was a cesspool of emotions.

"Something wrong?" Carter handed me a beer.

"No. Just wondering why we always promise to come here last, yet we always end up here first."

"Bad habit." He tucked a strand of hair behind my ear. "What's really wrong?"

"Nothing..." I lied. "Nothing at all."

"Carter! Arizona!" Josh walked over, clearly buzzed within an inch of his life. "What are you two doing here? No, wait. Don't answer that."

"You guys want to bar hop with us?" The girl hanging on his shoulder asked. "We're going to head down to 13th Street and try to make it back down here within two hours."

"All cover charges are on me!" Josh made an offer we couldn't refuse.

We left the bar, walking through the city's balmy night air. I shivered when we made it several blocks down and immediately felt Carter placing his blazer over my shoulders.

"You know what's going to be funny five to six years from now?" Josh asked as we stood in line at Club Red."

"What?"

"When one of you gets married. If it's you, Carter, you're going to have to explain to your wife that wherever Ari goes, you go. And I'm not sure if she's going to take that very well."

"Okay." Carter shook his head. "Just how many drinks have you had tonight?"

"I'm practically sober." Josh laughed. "But seriously though. Now that we're done with college and out in the real world, just think about that. I seriously don't think you two going to singles clubs together is going to be a good move anymore."

"You two aren't a couple?" His date spoke up. "Didn't I see you two at the EPIC house party together?"

"No, no, no…" Josh said. "They're together wherever they go. Don't even try to question anything. It's the weirdest friendship I've ever seen so just roll with it like I do. Guess what the best part about it is, though?"

"What?" She looked utterly intrigued.

"They've never even thought about crossing the line," he said. "Known each other since fifth grade—"

"Fourth grade," I corrected him.

"Okay, fourth grade," he said. "Yet they've never even so much as kissed each other. If I was a sap and they weren't my friends, I'd actually think the idea is kind of sweet…"

"It is!" She laughed. "Okay, I must have seen two other people all over each other at the party. That's cool…Strictly friends minus the attraction? I like that."

"I like it, too." Josh said. "Let me know if one of your spouses ever tries to claim you're cheating via a divorce. I'd be more than happy to volunteer to be your lawyer."

"Thanks…" We managed in unison.

Josh handed the bouncer a twenty, and after the man checked all of our IDs, we headed straight for the bar. Josh started a tab and encouraged us to "live it up," and I realized why he was being so generous: 1) He'd been accepted to intern at the number one law firm in the city; 2) He was trying to get laid. ASAP.

From the looks of things, it was definitely going to happen.

The four of us moved from club to club—drinking, laughing, dancing recklessly. Every now and then, I felt Carter's not-so-subtle touches in public: His hand on my hips whenever I danced, his fingers brushing against mine whenever we walked. And each time our eyes met, I felt my heart flip, felt it beat at a faster pace.

By the time we reached the seventh bar, Josh and his date had long abandoned us and we were tossing back weak shots alone.

"You have to tilt your head back, Ari." Carter tilted my chin up. "Otherwise you won't get the full effect of the liquor "

"I'm knocking back cranberry juice." I laughed. "There is no effect."

"All of those are cranberry juice?"

"Yeah. Someone has to drive." I pointed to the three large drinks in front of him. "We can't both be inebriated."

He looked at me a long time, slowly shaking his head. "They're all Cranberry juice as well."

"You're not drunk? Not tipsy in the slightest?"

"No…"

"Then… Since Josh left us, are you ready to go?"

"I thought you'd never ask." He stood up and took my hand, leading me out and down the street. "My place or yours?"

"Yours…" I clasped his hand behind the gear shift and we rode to his place in silence.

When he pulled into the driveway, he looked over at me. "What time is your flight Friday?"

"Ten in the morning," I said, knowing he already knew the answer to that question.

"What day are you unpacking everything and repacking it with a spreadsheet?"

I smiled. "Tomorrow."

"Will you need help?"

I nodded.

"Okay." He cut off the engine. "I'll be there."

Silence.

He got out of the car and opened my door, leading me inside his house for what was probably the last time this summer. When we made it to his room, I took off the blazer he'd given me and opened my purse.

"I meant to give this to you weeks ago." I pulled out the blue box my room-mates wanted me to pass along. "It's a farewell present since they consider you a roommate, too."

"Is it a bill for all the groceries I've eaten?" He untied the ribbon on top, and held up the small silver necklace that read, Arizona's Best Friend Forever. "This is very cute, but I'm pretty sure I'll never wear this…"

"They gave me one, too." I laughed. "It says Carter's Best Friend Forever…She said they were drunk when they picked these out."

"Clearly…" He set the necklace on his dresser and pulled me close, running his fingers through my hair.

Looking into his eyes, I wanted to use our last full night together to tell him how I felt about him, to hear him say the same, but I couldn't get the words out.

Instead, I took the safe approach. "Do you know that I've gotten used to you always being a few blocks, or a few miles away? You being accessible no matter what?"

"What makes you think I don't feel the same way?"

"Do you?"

"Yes," he said, kissing my lips. He slowly pulled my shirt over my head and unfastened my jeans.

I returned the favor, pulling his shirt over his head, unbuckling his belt.

Smiling, he picked me up and set me on the bed—slowly pulling the pants from my legs. I kept my eyes on his as he took his off, as he joined me in bed and immediately kissed my lips—not letting me control the tempo.

He kissed me and I shut my eyes—letting him caress every inch of my skin, listening to him whisper my name in between breaths. Within seconds, he pulled me on top of him and positioned me over his cock, slowly pushing me onto it. Grabbing my hips, he slowly rocked me back and forth—all while keeping his eyes on mine.

I pressed my hands against his chest, feeling the words "I love you" on the tip of my tongue, but soft moans came out instead.

I collapsed, falling forward and he slowly slipped out of me.

Catching my breath, I felt him getting out of bed. I wanted to ask where he was going, but he came right back, pulling me against his chest and kissing my forehead.

Neither of us spoke for a long time. We just looked into each other's eyes.

"I'm going to miss you," he said. "So fucking much."

"If we hadn't ever had sex would you feel the same?"

"Very much so…You're the only person I talk to almost every day."

"Unless you have a girlfriend."

"No." He blew a strand of hair away from my face. "I still talk to you the same amount even then."

"That's probably why they all hate me."

He grinned, kissing me again. "Probably." He rolled me off of him and trailed his finger down my side, stopping when he reached my tattoo—a small silver key.

"When did you get this?"

"The same night we got tattoos in eleventh grade."

"I've never noticed it before."

"I've never had a reason to get naked around you before."

"Hmmm. What does it mean?"

"It means I was drunk and asked for a key, so the technician asked me to describe the type I wanted, and when I couldn't, he just did his own thing."

"How deep and insightful…Tell me something you've never told me before…" His hand continued to trail down lower, to my thigh.

"I don't think there's anything I've never told you before."

"There has to be something." He kissed my lips. "It doesn't have to be anything major…"

"You might've been partially right about the bush thing with Scott, although I was, in fact. getting bad vibes that had absolutely nothing to do with that…"

"Sure it didn't." He smiled. "And once again, for the record, no guy really cares about that…" He glanced down at my legs. "Although, I do enjoy the bare look."

I rolled my eyes, blushing. "Your turn. Tell me something you haven't told me before."

"I hated you in third grade, too."

"You didn't even know me in third grade!" I laughed. "Be serious."

"I wanted to finish what we started at the EPIC party. I wanted to have you against the wall."

"How romantic."

"You didn't say it had to be romantic," he said. "I am being serious, though…"

"Okay, wait. I just thought of something you've never told me about."

"Doubt it, but what do you think that is?"

"Elliot in eleventh grade. He didn't come to school for two weeks after my disaster date with him, after you picked me up that night. Any idea why?"

"Nope." He smirked. "No idea at all."

"You do know why!" I looked into his eyes. "Tell me!"

"What do I get in return?"

"Not sure, but I'll leave if you don't comply…"

"So, this is a threat?"

I nodded. "A very serious one. Tell me…"

"After I got my car back the next day, I called Josh and told him I needed his help with something—told him some guy had mistreated you and I didn't appreciate it."

"And?"

"And we found him and beat the shit out of him. He should've never left you alone like that..." He trailed my lips with his fingers. "Anything could've happened to you..."

My jaw dropped, but I quickly recovered. "He never told on either of you?"

"We gave him plenty of incentive not to." He smiled. "He deserved it."

"I can't believe you did that..."

"Believe it," he said. "I wouldn't lie to you."

Okay, say it now. Say, I think I love you...Say, I think I'm in love with you...I love you, Carter, I—

His lips were on mine again and my mind lost the thought—deciding to focus on the last few hours of our time together instead of wasting it with more words...

twelfth grade

Carter

Subject: Truth or Dare
   Pick one.
   Sincerely,
   Carter

Subject: Re: Truth or Dare.
   Dare.
   Intrigued,
   Arizona

Subject: Re: Re: Truth or Dare.
   I dare you to tell me what really happened between you and Matt last night.
   Sincerely,
   Carter

Subject: Re: Re: Re: Truth or Dare
   I picked DARE. That's a TRUTH. That's cheating! But since we're speaking of Matt...Gah! I should've said no to being his date tonight. Why is he wearing a yellow tuxedo?

Embarrassed,
Arizona

Subject: Awaiting the Dare...
You were definitely better off coming to prom alone. I'm starting to think I should've done the same.
My date keeps asking me questions about when I plan on becoming a professional athlete. Tell me what happened between you and Matt, or, actually tell me anything. I need some intelligent conversation. My date doesn't speak much.
Sincerely,
Carter

Subject: Re: Awaiting the Dare
Meet me at the punch bowl in fifteen minutes.
You're welcome (in advance) for the distraction,
Arizona

I walked over to the punch bowl minutes later and met Arizona. "I've got five minutes before she notices I've been away too long."

"I've got ten." She grabbed my hand and pulled me out of the ballroom.

She tugged on all the doors as we walked down the hallway, until she finally found one that would open: A janitor's closet.

"We needed to have the conversation in here?" I asked. "Are we in grade school again? Twilight zone, maybe?"

"It was awful." She slumped against a small chair. "Absolutely awful."

"What are you talking about?"

"Losing my virginity." She shook her head. "I'm hoping the next time will be better..."

"There aren't any do-overs on virginity That's…not how that works."

She rolled her eyes. "I meant sex. I figure he'll try to do it again tonight, and I've heard some girls say it gets better with time so I can only hope."

"I hope it's better for you, too…" I sighed. "Sorry it wasn't what you thought it would be."

"It's not your fault…" She looked up at me. "So, when do you plan on telling the media hounds what college you're attending? You know all of those greedy-eyed recruiters are waiting with bated breath."

"You're not?"

"Why would *I* be?"

"Because I haven't told you either."

"But I know you so I'm pretty sure it's an easy guess."

"Out of forty six schools with full scholarship offers on the table?" I crossed my arms. "Try me."

"When I get this right, you owe me a trip to Martha's Waffle Place. Your treat."

"When you get this wrong, I'll take you to the IHOP down the street."

She smiled. "South Beach University."

I was silent.

"Is that it?" she asked. "Did I get it right?"

"Nope."

"Liar!" She laughed. "I can see it all over your face. "You should accept the facts by now. I know you better than you know yourself."

"No, you just think that you do."

"Want to bet on that, too?"

"As a matter of fact—" I stopped talking as the doorknob turned, as the door suddenly opened.

In walked Mr. Florence, the same janitor from years past. He looked back and forth between Ari and me, shaking his head.

"Thank you," he said. "Thank you both very much for being the perfect sign that I really do need to retire...Now, get the hell out of my closet..."

track 20. all you had to do was stay (4:49)

Carter

had a feeling in my chest when I woke up this morning that I was going to regret this goodbye for the rest of my life. I didn't try to stop it, though. Didn't attempt to question or wonder why this unfamiliar feeling had suddenly appeared. I just went through the motions.

I got dressed early, drove to the airport to meet Arizona, and ignored whatever that unwelcome feeling was.

"Are you sure you can't go with her?" Ari's mom stood by my side at the terminal. "Just to make sure she gets there safely?"

"Mom..." Ari said. "People fly all the time. I'm pretty sure I'll be okay."

I hadn't told Ari, but her mom had called me every day this week—asking me to do small things that helped lessen her OCD-like worries: I printed information about the type of airliner Ari would be flying on, the last known accident on the aircraft. I even managed to look up who the pilot would be and tell her he had a stellar record and hadn't been in any accidents.

"I need the two of you to take a picture together..." she said. "I need to remember this moment."

I walked over to Ari and put my arm around her shoulder. We both held our smiles, looking right at her mom as she clicked the button, but nothing happened.

"Ugh!" She slapped her forehead with her palm. "I forgot to buy new batteries for this thing. I'll be right back. Don't move." She stepped away and walked to a gift-shop.

Ari looked up at me and sighed. "Can I ask you something?"

"Anything."

"Do you think I'm making the right choice?" Her voice cracked. "Is this the right choice?"

"What do you mean?"

"Like...Three weeks ago, I was going to Cleveland for culinary school. I was still going to be in the States and I could have flown home once a month...maybe more. But two weeks ago everything changed and I just...I don't know anymore. Do you think going abroad to this school is what's best for me?"

"It's the second highest ranked culinary school in the world, correct?"

She nodded.

"Then I don't think you need me to tell you it's the right choice..."

"I'm just wondering if..." Her voice trailed off. "Never mind... My chest feels like it's going to explode any minute because I've had anxiety ever since I woke up this morning...Just so you know, I still expect you to email me whenever you get a chance so I won't have to use so many international minutes, and you have to write me one letter a month."

"Via email?"

"No, a real letter like old times."

"It's going to take a week or two for it to get to you."

"I don't care. I want one. I think it's going to feel weird enough not talking to you so much."

"Doubt it. I won't notice your absence at all."

She hit my shoulder. "You'll miss me more than I miss you."

"Want to bet?"

"Twenty dollars."

"That's all I'm worth?"

"That's all you're getting." She laughed and leaned close.

I ran my fingers through her hair, suddenly feeling the need to kiss her lips, to pull her close and give her a kiss she'd never forget in front of everyone around us.

Fuck it... I covered her mouth with mine, claiming every inch of it with my tongue—not letting her go when she pretended like she wanted to. I bit her bottom lip, and smiled as she murmured against my mouth, but when I felt like she needed to take a breath, I finally pulled away.

Staring at me in shock, her cheeks turned red—a mix of horniness and anger.

"Add that to the list of shit that never happened between us..." I said under my breath, gently rubbing her back. "For the record, you're doing the right thing by chasing your dreams...You know that, and you should—"

"I love you." She cut me off. "I'm in love with you, and I need you to know that...I think I've loved you for most of my life, and...Even though I'm going away today, I need to know if...I need to know if you feel the same."

Silence.

Her last paragraph repeated itself in my mind on a loop: I love you, I'm in love with you, do you feel the same...

I knew what I should've said, what would make her flight easier, but I had to say what I knew was better. What I knew was the right thing to do.

"Ari..." I said, looking into her eyes.

"Yes?"

"I'm sorry…" I noticed tears welling in her eyes. "Please don't take this to heart but…I do love you, I love you very much but…"

"But?" Her face fell. "But, *what*?"

"But not in that way…You're my best friend and I know we had sex but…We're just friends."

Wiping away a stray tear, she forced a smile and nodded, stepping back. "Right…Just friends."

I reached out and pulled her back. "You're doing the right thing by going abroad. You're going to kick ass."

"Thank you　" She gave me a hug and we stood still in an awkward embrace before slowly breaking apart.

"Did I miss something?" Her mom walked back over, looking between us both. "Why is your face so red, Ari?"

"I have no idea." She turned away from me.

Her mom looked between the two of us again but didn't press any further. "Could you stand next to each other again?"

We stepped closer and she snapped shot after shot.

"Okay…How about a hugging pose?" She snapped again. "Give each other a real hug! Like you're actually best friends who won't see each other for a while. Ari, you look like you don't even want to be around Carter right now…"

If only she knew…

When she was satisfied with our less than stellar shots, she snapped her fingers and made solo requests for just Ari.

"Could you go stand by that departure sign, Ari?" Her mom asked. "Oh, and I need to get one of you in front of the international sign, too."

Ten minutes later, when her mom had managed to snap a photo of her at every angle, Ari gave us both a hug.

"Take care, you two," she said. "I love you both…Very, very much…"

"Love you, too," we said.

"They're going to start boarding in about thirty minutes…" She looked at her watch. "I need to get through security." Her eyes met mine. "Talk to you later?"

"Talk to you later."

She walked away and I kept my eyes on her until she disappeared. I walked her mom—who started to cry, back to her car, and when I was sure she wasn't too emotional to drive, I headed to my car.

As I was starting the engine, I felt my phone vibrating. A text from Ari.

"How much did you spend on upgrading me to first class?"

"I didn't upgrade you to first class."

"Someone did…I didn't pay for this."

"You did. Your seat was always 2A."

"Ha! I knew it. Thank you very much…"

"No problem. I figured ten-plus hours in economy class would've brought out the worst in you and your anxiety. Be safe."

"Okay."

"Okay."

I drove off and when I stopped at a red-light, I saw that she'd sent me another text.

"Okay so…Just to be clear because well…I don't know. Sometimes you push people away when you don't want to show emotions…When we were having sex…You felt nothing? It was just sex?"

"You putting it that way makes me sound like an asshole, Ari…"

"I didn't say you were an asshole. Just tell me."

"Yes. It was just sex."

"Okay. Talk to you later."

"Talk to you later."

track 21. should've said no (2:44)

Arizona

I couldn't stop crying.

My heart felt heavy, and no matter how many times I wiped away my tears, more of them fell down my face. A part of me wished that I was sitting in coach and not first class so it would be easier to hide my pain, so flight attendants wouldn't be so accessible and could stop offering me endless drinks and looks of sympathy.

I started to wonder if the heartbreak was written all over my face, if the other passengers in my cabin could see it.

Carter's words, "I'm sorry...I love you, but not in that way," wouldn't stop replaying themselves in my head, and I couldn't stop staring at his last text: "Yes. It was just sex." I was hoping that the words were playing a cruel joke on me, because I still couldn't believe he felt differently than I did...

I'd thought the way he looked at me when we made love meant something, that the way he treated me (better than anyone he'd ever dated) was indicative of something more. Something much more between us.

"Here you go..." A flight attendant set another packet of Kleenex in my lap. "Would you like another cup of juice?"

"No..." I sniffled. "I'm..." I paused. I would probably never see her or any of the people on this plane again in my life. "Can I have two glasses of your hardest liquor? Actually, can you make that four?"

She looked as if she was going to recite some company line, but she smiled instead. "Be right back."

Turning to face the window, I stared at the wing of the plane as it cruised through clouds. I hoped that four glasses of alcohol would be enough for me to sleep through the remaining hours of this flight without dreaming.

Then again, if I did, I hoped that the images would show me going back in time and not talking to Carter as much. Maybe if we'd never had the opportunity to cross the line, this never would have happened.

I scrolled through my memories with him, pinpointing one that would've definitely prevented my heartbreak. It wasn't erasing any of our nightly phone calls or the emails, or hanging around him when we were in high school; it was making the decision to go to a college near his.

I should've never done that...

freshman year

Carter

Subject: Star Status

Dare I ask how many women you've attempted to sleep with since you've started the semester? If I see another commenter on Facebook talk about how "sexy" you are on your profile picture, I will scream. (Why are you using that picture of us anyway? And what the hell is up with that CAPTION???!!)

Arizona

Subject: Re: Star Status

The word "attempt" implies that I actually have to try to sleep with someone here. I don't. You're only upset because none of the commenters are leaving compliments about you. (I like that picture of us in eleventh grade. No one will ever know what "Beat her to it…Best twenty dollars I ever won" means…)

Sincerely,

Carter

I put my phone away and focused on the girl who was sitting at my table.

Earlier today, she'd claimed to have no idea who I was, but the first question out of her mouth was, "Do you think you'll go pro after college?"

Hell no... "Anything is possible," I'd responded. "I'm only focusing on the present."

Now, our main conversation points were all used up, and I was just waiting for her to get to the inevitable ending for our night.

"So..." she said. "When you're not hanging out with your basketball friends, who do you hang out with?"

"Myself, really," I said. "I don't really have time for much else."

She frowned and stood up, moving so she could sit right next to me. "That's so sad...You don't have any real friends? People outside of your teammates?"

"Not at the moment, but I'm sure I'll make some eventually."

"Why not start with *me*?" She bit her lip and rubbed my thigh under the table. "As a matter of fact, I think you and me can be *best friends*."

"Becoming best friends takes a lot of time." My cock hardened as she caressed it through my pants. "I'm not sure I'll have much of that when the season starts."

"You have to sleep somewhere at night, right?" She bit her lip again. "I'll be there for you whenever you need me...Want me to show you how good it could be, future best friend?"

"I would." I smiled. "Tell me when."

"Tonight?"

"Tonight works."

"Okay." Satisfied with my answer, she smiled wider and got up. "I'm going to tell my friends I'm leaving. You think you'll be ready to go by the time I get back?"

"Most definitely."

She blushed and walked away, and I signaled to the waitress for the check. Then I pulled out my phone, noticing another email from Arizona.

Subject: Scheduling Time.

Now that you're going to be a huge basketball star, I guess I'll have to start making appointments to come see you. How far out into the year are you booked with groupies? Or do I need to go through your "people" for things like this?

Rolling my eyes,
Arizona

Subject: Re: Scheduling Time.

You wouldn't have to make appointments to see me at all if you'd chosen to go to a closer school. You hate snow and rain, so you should've never agreed to go the University of Pittsburgh.

Sincerely,
Carter

Subject: Re: Re: Scheduling Time.

I know...Which is why I just transferred. Well, THAT and other stupid things...Ugh. I know it's sad that I only lasted a month, but I couldn't stand the dreariness, and that professor I was adamant about learning from? Apparently he got this huge book deal before the semester started and is stepping down from teaching for two years so he can finish it.

Please don't tell me 'I told you so'...
Regretting things,
Arizona

Subject: Re: Re: Re: Scheduling Time.

I fucking told you so.
Sincerely,
Carter

PS—What school are you transferring to?

Subject: Re: Re: Re: Re: Scheduling Time.
Reeves University. Seven minutes away from your precious South Beach University.
I'm actually here right now unpacking. God, I missed the beach!
Will call you when I get more done.
Arizona

Subject: Re: Re: Re: Re: Re: Scheduling Time.
No need. I'll come help you. Send me your address.
Sincerely,
Carter

I wrote a "something came up" on a napkin for my "future best friend," and headed straight to the address Ari texted me. It was exactly seven minutes like she said, and just like my dorm, it was steps away from the beach. Unlike my dorm though, where everyone had a roommate, it seemed as if all the suites in Ari's dorm were singles.

I didn't bother knocking on her already open door. "Ari?"

"I'm back here!" She yelled.

I stepped past the closet and saw her folding clothes on the bed.

"Why didn't you tell me you were here? I would've helped you move your stuff." I asked.

"Because the week I made my decision, you were on ESPN's college channel with your team-mates talking about how explosive a season this was going to be, how many intensive practices you were looking forward to. I figured you'd be busy. No practice today?"

"No." I looked around her room. "I just had a date."

"How'd it go?"

"If I'm here talking to you, how do you think it went?"

She threw a pillow at my face. "Nice seeing you again, too! You want to make yourself useful and actually help me unpack? Could you unload all my books?"

"Sure." I opened the labeled box and started sorting them. "Within the entire month that you wasted in Pittsburgh, did you do anything worth talking about?"

For the next few hours, we caught up on all the little details that'd slipped through emails and text messages, all the insignificant things that were now seemingly important. And by the end of the night, we'd almost unpacked most of her things.

"Are there any good places to eat on campus?" she asked, yawning. "If not, would you mind driving back to our neighborhood so we can eat at Sam's?"

"There's actually this place called Gayle's I think you'll like."

"*Gayle's*? It sounds like an old fashioned diner "

"It is, but the food is perfect. They serve just as many flavors of yogurt as they do of ice cream, and their waffles are ten times better than Sam's."

"I refuse to believe that…Do they have a candy bar?"

"They do."

"What about breakfast at all hours of the day?"

"Definitely."

"Okay, fine." She smiled. "I'm sold, but if I don't like it, you have to pay."

"I was going to pay anyway…" I pulled out my car keys. "Let's go."

———

Minutes later, we were seated in a booth at Gayle's—arguing over stupid things like old times and looking over the extensive dessert menu.

"So, is this why you've been turning down every girl that approaches you in here, Carter?" The only waitress I'd ever seen in this place stepped in front of us. "Is this your girlfriend?"

"Ha! *Never.*" Ari laughed. "I'm Arizona. His best friend."

"Since fifth grade," I said.

"Fourth grade, Carter." Ari countered. "It was *fourth grade.*"

"No, I couldn't stand you in fourth grade."

"Well, I personally can't stand you sometimes now, but it still counts as us being friends doesn't it?"

"Best friends, huh?" The waitress rolled her eyes. "Okay…I'll buy that for now…What do you want to order?"

"A Belgian waffle with vanilla yogurt and strawberries—with a sprinkle of chocolate chips," Ari said.

"A waffle tower with chocolate yogurt, peanut butter, and a sprinkle of Oreo chips and candy on the side" I said, waiting for her to walk away. "For the record Ari, just so we're clear, it was definitely fifth grade."

"Are you really going to start an argument with me over this?" She crossed her arms. "Do you really think I'll ever let you win this? It was fourth grade, Carter. Fourth. Grade."

"I've got all night…"

track 22. two is better than one (3:58)

Carter

Subject: Landed
> *In France. Talk to you soon.*
> *Arizona.*
> *PS—I have my international minutes but no adapter to charge my phone. Sigh. I'll call you after I figure out where to buy one...*

Subject: Re: Landed
> *Glad you had a safe flight.*
> *Sincerely,*
> *Carter*
> *PS—Looking forward to talking.*

She never called.

Never emailed, either.

It'd been three weeks since our last email exchange, three weeks since I last kissed her lips, and life without her at home was taking a lot more time to get used to than I'd originally anticipated. Our usual weekends together at the beach became moments alone for me to study. Our emails about the little things became nothing at all. And instead of buying her breakfast at Gayle's all the time, I was buying it for our own waitress who, ironically, had never eaten the diner's food.

I was waking up every morning—reaching for her, rolling over in bed at night to pull her closer, but she was never there. That ache in my chest from the day at the airport intensified each day she didn't call, and a part of me was starting to wonder if I'd said the right thing at all...

I checked my email and physical mailbox incessantly, hoping to hear something—*anything*, and after not being able to take it anymore, I decided to pen my letter first...

three weeks gone

Carter

Dear Arizona,

  I haven't heard from you since you landed, so I hope you don't mind that I'm writing you first. I'm not sure when exactly you'll get this, and since it's been a while since I actually wrote one of these by hand, I'll try to do my best...

  Law school will be starting in a month, and you'll be proud (and slightly shocked, I'm sure) to know that I completed all of the required reading and turned in all of the required reports already. Josh has yet to start reading the first book, but he's assured me that he'll get it done somehow...

  Since you're not here, I've been treating our usual waitress to Gayle's instead. How ironic is it that she's never eaten there/never really wanted to? She's hooked now, though. She's also told me that the owner is considering renovating the place to make it bigger for the onslaught of tourists. If he does, I'll send you pictures.

  Speaking of pictures, here are a few of the beach and a few of the ones we took at the marina together before you left...

Not sure what else I should say right now, but I miss you (a lot...) and hope you'll come home for that fall break that your school gives you. I also hope you'll respond to at least one of my emails...I've sent you quite a few...

Write back and tell me how everything is going with you.

Hope you're okay.

I really do miss you...

Sincerely,

Carter

Dear Carter,

I am okay. Glad to hear you are well.

Thanks for your letter,

Arizona

Dear Arizona,

Did you seriously waste an international stamp and three weeks of shipping time to send me that short ass letter? (Also, do you still not have internet? Can you not answer emails?)

Sincerely,

Carter

Dear Carter,

I apologize for the brevity of my last letter. It wasn't intentional, I promise. I appreciate the photos you sent (I hung them up on my wall) and I wasn't shocked that you finished your required reading in advance at all. (You got a 180 on the LSATs...I would be more shocked if you didn't get it done.)

I am actually quite miserable here and I think I might've taken that out on you a little bit, so I'm sorry. The classes here are super intense, from six in the morning until six in the evening, and after that we're required to attend workshops that can last anywhere between four and five hours, so I usually just pass out.

I ordered a charger for my phone from amazon.com, but they sent me the wrong one by mistake. Two times in a row, so I'm hoping the correct one arrives soon.

My roommate is a jerk who barely talks to me so I've decided to ignore her altogether.

I don't really have much else to say, but I promise to call you and do better with emails...

Thanks for your letter,

Arizona

track 23. treacherous (3:39)

Arizona

I can't do this...
I logged into my email account and saw that Carter had sent me over fifty new emails since I'd come to France. My mouse hovered over the first message—Subject: Truly Missing My Best Friend, but I couldn't open it.

It'd been hard enough responding to that first letter of his—that generic "Let's just act like nothing ever happened between us" bullshit, so I shut off my computer and got into bed.

My days were now a lot shorter without talking to him, a lot less memorable and trivial, too. But I couldn't sacrifice my heartache in exchange for empty conversations between us. Not now.

I needed to think long and hard about everything before I sent him any more correspondence...

track 24. half of my heart (4:15)

Arizona

Subject: Phone Update.

Dear Carter,

I tried calling you earlier, but the static in my flat is so bad that the call never went completely through...I'm actually typing this email from an internet café in town since the internet in my flat is even worse.

Anyway, our program is about to kick into even higher gear than before, and even though I have a charger now, I'll have little time to take breaks during the week to talk.

I just want you to know that I'm not avoiding or ignoring you.

I hope you are well, and I'll do my best to send you physical letters as much as I can...

Also, thank you for mailing me those tins of waffle batter from Gayle's. I truly appreciate it.

Looking forward to talking to you when I get a break.

Sincerely,

Arizona

Eighty percent of that email was a lie.

My flat had perfect internet. My phone service, even better.

And I was ahead in all my classes so I had ample time to take breaks. The only thing that was true was my appreciation for the waffle batter; I'd made half of it the first week I received it.

I hit send on my lie-filled email to Carter and changed my email settings, making sure that any future messages from him would go directly into my spam folder.

I'd still been crying myself to sleep every night, no matter how hard I tried not to. In class, I was poised and focused—eager to soak up anything that would take my mind off of 'not in that way,' but once I was left alone, without structures and rigorous lessons, I fell apart.

Several times, I even tried to respond to one of his handwritten letters, but the only words that came out were curse words.

Even worse, I felt like the two of us were so fucking close that I had nobody else I could talk to about this. He was literally all I had.

I started to log off the internet, but I saw Nicole's "online" symbol light up in my video chat sidebar and clicked "connect" without thinking twice.

The screen read "connecting soon" and within minutes her face appeared on my screen.

"Well, hey there, stranger!" She smiled.

"Hey…" I managed.

"I've been trying to connect with you for the longest! I didn't even know you'd left so soon until I heard it from Carter…You could've at least said goodbye."

I stared blankly at her.

"Ari?" She asked, looking confused. "Ari, why are you looking like that? Can you hear me?"

"Yes…Yes, I can hear you."

"Okay, then." She smiled again. "Well, how are you? How's France? How are you holding up without Gayle's and having your BFF around all the time?"

I couldn't hold it in anymore.

"I slept with Carter..." I burst into tears and my chest heaved up and down. "I slept with him damn near every day after the EPIC party..."

Her jaw dropped.

"I didn't think it was 'just sex' though," I continued, feeling the tears fall nonstop. "I thought I was falling in love with him because I thought I thought he was..." My next words came out muddled and I shook my head. "I can't eat, I can't sleep, and I can't even think straight anymore..."

"It took so much out of me to finally tell him that I was in love with him, and I honestly thought he would say that he loved me back...But he said, 'I love you, but *not* in that way'...He said that in his eyes, we were just friends. That the sex didn't mean anything more..."

Nicole looked completely shocked, dumbfounded, and I didn't stop talking. I couldn't.

"I've been crying every day since I got here, Nicole. Every. Fucking. Day. On the one hand, I've cried because of the situation, because it hurts not to be loved back. But on the other, it's because I really *really* want to talk to him, you know?"

"*Awww, Ari...*"

"I want to tell him about the stuff I've seen, tell him he should come up so I can give him a tour of what little I know and..." I wiped my face on my sleeve. "But I can't just be his friend anymore, not right now anyway. I can't talk to him like we used to because I don't want him thinking I'm okay. I am NOT okay, and I will not pretend like I am..."

Nicole was silent for a long time—her eyes meeting mine, waiting for me to give her a look that said it was okay for her to speak.

"Ari, I'm so sorry..." She paused. "Actually, before I address any of what you just said, I want to apologize to you for something I did."

I raised my eyebrow, confused.

"It hit me last week when your phone kept going to voicemail or when you hadn't answered in a long time that I was a terrible friend to you. I was too busy chasing guys that never lasted for more than a few nights at a time, instead of being there for you…I was in the middle of sending you an email that said all of this stuff tonight, but I really do want to do better now and in the future."

"Thank you…"

"As far as Carter…" she said. "I need to get to the most important question out of the way…"

"What question is that?"

"How big is his cock?" She asked, deadpan, and I laughed for the first time in what felt like forever.

"It's big *Huge*, actually."

"I knew it…" She fanned herself and bit her lip. "Lucky you. Anyway, you don't have to talk to him until you're ready. He'll just have to understand. Whenever you do talk to him, though, you have to be honest and tell him everything and how he made you feel. You have to also be willing to accept that you two may not be able to be friends again. At least, not for a while."

"Yeah…" My heart ached at the very thought. "That's what hurts the most to think about…"

"If it makes you feel any better, I ran into him last weekend at a party and he looked absolutely miserable."

"Why do you think that would make me feel better?"

"I just thought it would." She shrugged. "He barely spoke to anyone and whenever a girl tried to dance with him, he walked away. Hell, when I told my friend that I was going to go talk to him, she told me to brace myself to be ignored or told to fuck off…He may actually feel the same way you do, and I'm willing to bet that he probably does love you in that way…"

"If he did, wouldn't he tell me? Wouldn't he write it in one of his letters since I'm currently avoiding his calls and emails?"

"Maybe." She shrugged. "Or maybe, just maybe, he's just as stubborn as you are…You are best friends for a reason."

"We *were* best friends for a reason. I hate him now."

"Ha!" She tilted her head to the side, laughing. "I'm sorry for laughing, but…Whether you talk to him this year or next year, it won't change the fact that you love him. You could never truly hate him."

"That's not true. You should've seen us in fourth grade."

"Is that so?" She was still laughing. "Something tells me you might've loved each other even then."

I shook my head, but I couldn't help but laugh with her.

Feeling slightly better, I steered the conversation away from Carter and asked about her life—attempting to pick up where we left off before.

She told me she was taking time off to study for the GMATs so she could go to grad school next year, and that she hadn't had a date in a while and was surprisingly enjoying the "studious life."

When we were done laughing about the sexual disaster that led to her hiatus, she promised to call me next week and we hung up.

I logged off of Skype and smiled. Shutting my laptop, I leaned over to turn off my lamp, but my roommate walked into my room and hit the main light switch.

"Okay, so…" she said. "Don't take this the wrong way, but I overheard most of your conversation with your friend from back home, and I think I actually like you now. You're not a bitch at all." She raised two coffee mugs. "Tea?"

track 25. come back...be here (2:58)

Carter

I refreshed my email inbox again and again, hoping for a reply, knowing there wouldn't be one.

I was sitting in a booth at The Book Bar, pretending to listen to my much older cousin, Sam. He was the only person in my shattered family that I talked to every now and then. He'd been there when I lost my father, when my mom walked away, and he'd made sure to come visit me at least twice a year, no matter how hectic his schedule was.

We'd been sitting in our booth for over an hour, though, and the only thing I'd paid attention to was our first hello. Everything after that was a blur.

"Carter?" He waved his hand in front of my face, getting my attention. "Are you in there? Are you listening?"

"Barely...My apologies. What were you saying?"

"Nothing." He shook his head. "But now that I have your attention, I think you need to get laid. How long has it been?"

"Who knows? Every day seems to be blending together these days."

"I warned you about law school, told you it was a kill-joy."

"Aren't *you* a lawyer?"

"We're all lawyers." He laughed. "I'm sure your dad is proud and looking down on you from above. He's probably beating his chest and yelling, 'That's my boy! The James' pride! The James' blood!'"

"My dad was so full of shit sometimes."

"He was." He sipped his beer. "What's the real reason you're looking like ass though? Usually when I come to see you, we go out and party. We haven't done shit so far, but hang out on the beach and drink."

"That sounds *so unfortunate…*"

"It is for someone like you. What's up? Please don't make me guess."

"You can try if you like."

"Okay, cool." He ordered another round of beers. "You don't really want to be a lawyer. You want to backpack across the world and shoot exotic porn for a living?"

"*What*? No…Law school is fine. I'm flying straight through it."

"Just checking." He laughed. "Okay, no wait. I've got it. Another girl dumped you for being an asshole?"

"Shockingly, no."

"Okay then… Another girl dumped you for talking to Arizona too much?"

My jaw clenched at the sound of Ari's name.

"*Again*, Carter?" He shook his head. "How many times are you going to keep making that mistake? The two of you really do talk way too much."

"That's not it." I signaled to the bartender for another drink.

"Well, if that's not it…What is it?"

"You said you were guessing."

"Right, um…I don't know, man. What, is Arizona mad at you about something?"

I nodded.

"Okay, so?" He laughed. "It's *Arizona*. She'll get over whatever it is eventually, I'm sure. It's not like you slept with her."

I said nothing.

His eyes met mine and he damn near choked on his beer. "Holy shit. You had sex with Ari?"

I didn't answer.

"You slept together, didn't you? Didn't you?"

"You do realize that you're asking the same exact question back to back, correct?"

"It's a habit of a courtroom lawyer." He slid me one of his beers and opened a new tab. "Anyway, when did this happen? Like, when did it start?"

"A few months ago."

"Hmmm." He shook his head. "Well, I honestly wish I could say I'm surprised but...I'm only surprised that it took you two this long to do it."

I glared at him. "You're not helping."

"I'm not here to help. I'm here to use you as a wingman and have fun. You're not helping with *that*..."

I raised my hand for another drink.

"Did you two only have sex once?" he asked.

"More than once," I said. *Way more than once...*

"There were no 'I finally see the light' or 'I love you's at the end?"

"No..."

"Why not?" He sipped his beer.

"I had my reasons..."

"Your *reasons*? Please. If it were anyone else, I might be able to swallow that. But you two?" He shook his head. "You're both too stupid to realize that you've been in love with each other your entire lives."

I gave him a blank stare.

"You don't believe me?" he asked.

"I don't have to. I'm pretty sure if I was in love with her for my entire life, I would've never dated anyone else…"

"One," he said, counting off on his fingers. "In sixth grade, she threw a birthday party and you were the only one who came."

"So?"

"So, for your birthday party, you only invited her to get back at all the people who dissed her the year before. You even gave her the invitation in front of everyone at school, including your 'first-kiss' girlfriend."

"I was just being a good friend."

"Two, you can't last in any relationship because you subconsciously compare every woman you date to Ari, even when you know you'll never be completely open with them if they do measure up."

"I have an unfortunate tendency to pick bat-shit crazy women. I never compare them to Ari."

"Three, if she calls you, you answer immediately and then you go running to wherever she is if she asks you to."

"Any best friend would do that."

"In the middle of a date? Or right after sex with his girlfriend?" He crossed his arms. "I don't think so."

I said nothing.

"That's what I thought. Now that you're somewhat accepting of the truth, do you want the most obvious fucking reason that you're in love with Arizona and always have been?"

"Not really."

He grabbed my arm and pointed to the small State of Arizona-shaped tattoo. "Any reason why you've never covered that or etched over it like any of your other ones? There's no sign or remnant of those old 'Carter and Jane' or 'Rose forever' tattoos anymore… "

"It's become a drunken memory. It makes for a good story."

"For *who*, Carter? No future wife or girlfriend is going to think that's a good story and you fucking know it."

I shrugged. "None of my previous girlfriends have ever complained to me about it before."

"That's because none of your previous girlfriends were ever smart enough to know all the states that make up America. They'd probably be shocked to know that there was one called Arizona in the first place."

I tried to think of a rebuttal, but I couldn't find one.

"You know what? Let's get out of here…" He actually sounded sympathetic. "You've got it bad, and I'm going to need a better wingman while I'm on this trip. Pussy whipped and love sick Carter is not going to help me at all…"

track 26. we are never ever getting back together (3:53)

Carter

More weeks passed and the beach's bipolar autumn—warm temperatures one day, unbearable rainfall the next, passed without incident. Without Arizona.

According to what her mom had told me, she didn't think it made much sense for her to spend over a thousand dollars on a plane ticket to come home for fall break. I didn't get a chance to offer to foot the bill because I was too engrossed in the hectic insanity of law school and I couldn't catch a break to save my life.

Everyone in my program operated on a cutthroat level and had already developed close knit study groups, so it left me with a lone study partner. Erica.

She was just as enthusiastic about the law as me: She'd scored a 180 on the LSATs as well, and her dad had influenced her into the career field, too.

"Hey. Do you want to split up the justice chapters again?" She tossed a few gummy bears in my direction. "Or maybe you just want to stare into space for a few more hours."

"We can split them up," I stood up and walked into my kitchen. "You want more coffee?"

"Yes, please."

I pulled out two mugs—noticing a new Post-It from Josh on the cabinet door: "There's absolutely no reason why you still haven't fucked Erica yet. That's the best way to get over Ari…Just do it."

I crumpled the note and threw it away.

"Can I ask you something, Carter?" Erica sat up on the couch.

"Anything."

"Are you dating someone?"

"I think you would know by now if I was. Don't you?"

"Not necessarily…" She blushed. "I mean, we do spend a lot of time together, but you always slip away for hours at a time on the weekends."

"To complete my internship hours." I smiled. "I'm pretty sure you do the same thing on the weekends."

"Oh, right…" she said and then, as I placed the coffee in front of her, she cleared her throat. "Would you like to go out sometime? Like, as friends? Nothing more than friends?"

I hesitated, finally looking her over and paying attention to her features. She was pretty—auburn colored hair, bright blue eyes, and if it weren't for a certain someone, I would've once considered her one of the most beautiful women I'd ever met. "Sure."

"Great! This weekend all of the first years are going to dinner and a movie downtown. Is that cool with you?"

"Perfect…Which chapters do you want me to outline?"

We worked side by side until nearly midnight, stopping after we'd gone through two more pots of coffee. I helped her put all her things back into her backpack and walked her outside to her car.

"We got a lot of work done today," she said, smiling as I held her car door open for her.

"We did. I'm sure we'll get the highest scores again, too."

"I'm sure…" She hesitated a second, and then she stood on her toes and planted a kiss on my cheek. "See you Saturday, Carter."

"See you Saturday…" I forced a smile and waited until she drove off before walking back inside. I was about to collapse on the couch and call it a night, but I spotted a letter on the TV stand. Addressed to me in Arizona's handwriting.

I quickly ripped it open and sat on the couch to read:

Dear Carter,

Sorry it took me so long to respond to your last letter, but unfortunately not much has changed in my life since we last wrote. (Or spoke…)

I still hate it here. It's absolutely beautiful despite the lack of beaches in the part of town I'm in, but that's about all I can say…

Anyway, who would've thought you would be number one in your class? I mean, I knew you'd do well, but that's amazing. Good for you. Maybe you can be my lawyer if I ever open up my own restaurant? (Funny how I've never given much thought to that before, but that'd be nice.)

Also, THANK YOU for sending me even more of those jars of Gayle's waffle batter. Believe it or not, I've used them all and I've got my classmates hooked on the crack that is Gayle's waffles. Well, that's it for me for now…Let me know how you're doing and I'll try to write back faster next time.

Sincerely,
Arizona

three months gone...and more

Carter

Dear Arizona,

I refuse to believe that you're not checking your emails at all.

I could maybe understand if you're reading them and quickly deleting them, but could you at least respond to one of the ones I sent you last week (or at least this letter. At least THIS goddamn letter so I know that you're reading what I send you...) whenever you get a chance. I need to talk to you about something important.

Not much has changed in my life here at home.

Still in law school.

Still number one in the class.

Still missing you. (More than I'll ever be able to explain.)

Sincerely,

Carter

Dear Arizona,

I need you to respond. Now.

Say something Anything.

Sincerely,

Carter

Dear Carter,

Happy Thanksgiving! I hope you enjoyed the holiday! (Please tell Josh I said hello!)

Sincerely,

Arizona

Dear Carter,

Merry Christmas! Hope Santa brought you everything you wanted and more! (Thank you for sending me more waffle batter from Gayle's! I've also mailed a separate "thank you" note just for that.)

Sincerely,

Arizona

Dear Carter!

HAPPY NEW YEAR! Whoa, crazy how the past six months have just flown by, huh? All is well here—I'm officially my teacher's favorite student and I think I might have a real female BFF in Nicole. (I think the distance made us stronger.)

Sincerely,

Arizona

track 27. begin again. (5:03)

Arizona

I dropped a few postcards into the mailbox for my mom one Saturday morning. I was slowly coming to terms with my new non-Carter filled life, and even though I still woke up some days feeling numb and occasionally broke down and cried in the middle of the night, I was faring way better than I was when I first got here.

I was making plenty of new friends in my classes, talking to Nicole once a week via Skype, and whenever I was feeling lonely, I wandered out to the coast.

Since there were no beaches here—only jagged rocks and rough waters that knocked against them, I would lay back against my blanket and shut my eyes—pretending I was back at home instead. I would envision sunny days and warm sand, and for once, I wouldn't be bothered by the tourists.

My plan for "make-believe beach" was derailed today, though. In my usual spot, a group of people dressed in grey tuxedos and pink dresses were preparing for a wedding, so I headed to a nearby café.

I ordered a pastry and a water, and sat by the window—trying my best to catch a glimpse of the ceremony, to see what true love looked like up close.

"Do you mind if I join you?" My classmate Sean, a gorgeous guy with green eyes and an American accent, suddenly stepped in my line of vision.

"I don't mind."

"Great." He held out a white mug. "Do you like orange blend?"

"Never had it." I took it from his hands and sipped it slow; it was amazing. "What are you doing here?"

"Tracking you down to see why you stood me up," he said, smiling. "We had a date yesterday. Did you forget?"

"*What*?" I raised my eyebrow, confused.

"You don't recall me saying that I'd pick you up from your flat at six for a night out?"

I remembered. I just didn't think he was serious, so I'd gotten into bed and gone to sleep early.

"I'm so sorry, Sean. I thought you were just joking."

He smiled and sat down, moving his chair close to mine. "Do you also think I'm 'just joking' when I call you every night and we talk on the phone for hours at a time? Or when I only ask *you* to stay behind after study sessions and we hang out all night at my place?"

I blinked, confused again.

"Arizona..." He leaned forward and ran his fingers through my hair. "I'm trying to *go out* with you... How else can I make that any clearer?"

I blushed, now feeling like a complete ditz. I'd thought nothing of our nightly phone conversations, weekend bike rides through town, or private study sessions.

"I just thought you were being a nice guy..." I said.

"I am a nice guy." His fingers were still in my hair. "Outside of the bedroom..."

My eyes widened and he laughed—leaning even closer.

"I don't know what else I can do to make you see that I'm interested," he said softly. "Tell me what it takes..."

I swallowed, looking him over. This was the second time in my life I'd failed to realize how sexy and attractive a guy was. With sun-kissed blond hair, deep green eyes, and a mouth that was too tempting not to try, he was definitely sexy as hell.

"Are you going to tell me?" he asked.

I hesitated. "What do you mean by *go out*?"

"I mean you'll actually hang out with me with the impression that I'm more than a nice guy." He looked into my eyes. "A guy who actually *likes* you…It also means you'll let me take you out to the city tomorrow."

"What if I'm busy tomorrow?"

"*If* implies that you're not, so I'll force you."

"How romantic…" I laughed. "Nonetheless, yes. I'll go out with you."

"Good…"he said, standing up and stepping back. "I'll pick you up at seven tomorrow."

"Wait," I called out. "You were kidding about that bedroom comment, weren't you?"

He looked over his shoulder and smirked. "I wasn't…"

Blushing, I watched him walk away and sat in the café a little longer, wondering if our day in Paris tomorrow would come with the cliché "falling in love atop the Eiffel Tower" moment. I knew one thing for sure though, I was starting a new compatibility spreadsheet for us; I needed to check off the "intensity of the kisses" category with him ASAP.

When I finally arrived back home, I noticed there was a new letter from Carter on my table.

I stared at it for a while, running my finger along the flap—along the words "URGENT: Please Open Me, Ari," but I couldn't bring myself to open it.

Just not right now…

track 28. how you get the girl (4:32)

Carter

"Mr. James," the postal employee sighed. "For the umpteenth time, we can't track letters, only packages. Would you like me to track your last package to France, maybe?"

"Bullshit. There has to be some way that you can track a goddamn letter..."

He rolled his eyes and motioned for me to step aside. "Next in line, please!"

Annoyed, I put my old receipt into my pocket and left the office. It'd been weeks since I sent Ari my last letter, and I'd sent it in a bright blue envelope with the words "URGENT: Please Open Me, Ari" across the back flap to make sure she'd have no choice but to read it. Yet, she hadn't sent one word back about it, and the only correspondence on her end had been generic holiday cards. With Valentine's Day a month and a half away, I wondered if she'd already made plans to send me another one of those.

As usual, when I got home, I checked the mail, not expecting anything from her inside of it. This time—to my surprise, there was. It was dated for two weeks ago, and her curly handwriting was all over the back flap.

I took it inside the house with me and immediately ripped it open:

Dear Carter,

I'm so sorry that it's taken me so long to write you an actual, personal letter back. Things have become quite hectic now—in both good and bad ways.

My roommate and I are on much better terms now (we're actually really, really good friends) and I still have the highest marks in my class. I am definitely living my dream—definitely sooo happy that I came here to this school, and I can't wait to cook you one of my gourmet breakfast dishes. (It's BETTER THAN GAYLE'S! And if it isn't, just tell me it is. LOL)

I'm not surprised to know that you're still number one in your cohort. I'll have to take you out to celebrate when I get home...

Speaking of which, I was going to surprise you but this letter will probably beat me there...I'm coming home for two whole weeks!!

See you soon.

Sincerely,

Arizona

What the fuck...

I shook the letter, flipped it to the back—reread it a few times, wondering if I'd missed a part. There was no mention of anything I'd sent her in my most recent letter. I was wondering if she'd read it and was simply evading the subject until she got home, or if she still hadn't read how I felt about the summer we spent together, how I felt about her.

I pulled out my phone to call Josh and tell him that I'd probably be spending the full two weeks with Arizona whenever she got here, but I noticed I had a missed call from Ari's mom.

Sighing, I called her back.

"Hey, Carter!" she answered on the first ring.

"Hello, Mrs. Turner."

"Mrs. Turner?" She laughed. "Really? You haven't called me that since you wrote me an 'I'm sorry for hurting your daughter's feelings' letter. You know better than that..."

I smiled. "Okay...*Second Mom*."

"Much better. I was calling to ask if you could do me a huge, *huge* favor."

"Anything."

"Ari's getting back home in about three hours according to the flight information she sent me."

She didn't think to tell me when her flight landed?

"Are you there, Carter?" her mom asked.

"I'm here."

"Well, I was going to ask if she could stay with you for just this weekend. I'm currently staying at a friend's because two of our water pipes burst and you know I refuse to step foot in there until it's all taken care of...If it's a problem, just let me know. I can see if maybe her new friend Nicole—"

"It's not a problem," I said, still silently seething at Ari's inability to tell me anything. "Should I pick her up from the airport, too?"

"Not at all! She's using my reward points for a free rental. I'll send her the text about the accommodation change, though. I'm sure she'll be thrilled to see you again."

"I'm sure..."

"Okay, got to go! I need to finish cleaning my friend's kitchen. Can you believe she didn't know to clean underneath her cabinets? She's been my best friend for all these years and I never had any idea about this. I wonder what else I don't know..."

"I know the feeling…"

"Talk to you later, Carter."

"Talk to you later." I hung up and took a seat on the couch, shaking my head and trying to process everything.

Her vague letter. Her not sending me an email with her flight information.

Her not acting like my friend.

Shit…

Unable to hold back, I sent her a text, "You couldn't at least send me an email with your flight information?"

I got a response a few hours later: "Sorry. It just slipped my mind…I saw my mom's text about staying at your place for the weekend…Are you at home now? Just landed. Pretty tired."

"I'm here."

"Okay. See you soon. On my way."

I took a deep breath and decided to clean up to clear my mind. I walked into the kitchen and put all the dishes away. In case she wanted to talk before going to sleep, I tossed a few pillows and blankets onto the couch, and by the time I'd made the bed in my room, there was a familiar light knock at my door.

I need you to listen to me for five minutes, Ari…Five minutes.

I silently repeated the words as I walked over and opened the door.

The second I laid eyes on her, I lost my train of thought.

She was fucking stunning. Dressed in simple jeans and a white T-shirt (one of my small, old T-shirts…), she'd cut her hair to shoulder length and added blond highlights.

"Hi…" She managed, slowly looking me up and down. Her hazel eyes slowly met mine and she forced a smile.

"Hi…"

We stood staring at each other for several seconds—neither of us attempting to shatter the silence. I leaned forward to take her bag from her hands, but she stepped back.

"This is my best friend Carter, Sean." She tilted her head to the guy who suddenly stepped from behind her, the guy I'd paid absolutely no attention to. "Carter, this is Sean. My boyfriend."

"Your *what*?"

"My boyfriend."

"Nice to meet you." Sean extended his hand to me, and I forced myself to shake it. "Do you mind if you let us in? I really need to lie down. We had a terrible flight, flying back in coach all the way here."

I opened my door wider, letting them in—keeping my eyes on Ari as she gave Sean a kiss on his cheek. Right in front of me. Right in fucking front of me.

"The bathroom is down that hall and to your left," she said, smiling at him. "Oh, and I guess these pillows and blankets are for us. You want blue or green?"

"Green." He kissed her on the cheek and walked away. "I'll be right back."

What. The. Fuck... "Ari..." I walked over to her and she ignored me, unfolding the blankets and setting up the pillows. "Ari...I know you hear me talking to you."

"I hear you."

"Is this Sean thing a joke? After all this time, are you playing a prank on me?"

"Why would someone fly from France to America as a joke? He really is my boyfriend."

"When did that happen?"

"About a month ago." She looked confused. "Didn't you get my letter?"

"This one?" I held up the one I'd just received today.

"No..." she said. "There was another one..."

"I would believe that, but you don't have the best track record with sending me shit. Did you get mine?"

"The one about hoping to see me and hang out again some-day? Or, was it the one that said, say something—anything, Ari? Please?"

"No…Not that one. Although, I must say it's good to know you were actually fucking reading what I wrote."

"Could you not curse at me like that?" She crossed her arms. "I haven't been home for five minutes and you're snapping at me?"

"I'm not snapping at you   I'm trying to figure out how you can literally go to another country for months, stop talking to me for no reason at all, and when you finally come back, not only do you not tell me in advance, but the first time that I see you again, you're dating someone else."

"*Someone else* implies that you and I were once dating, that we were in some type of intimate relationship…" She narrowed her eyes at me. "And I had a really good reason for not talking to you."

"Care to share it?"

"Not particularly. "She looked like she was trying to stay as calm as possible. "We weren't dating, Carter. We were just friends, remember?"

I felt my blood pressure rising, but I said nothing. Instead I looked her over again—trying to figure out who she was right now. This wasn't the Arizona I knew at all.

"This is a really nice place, Carter." Sean walked into the room. "Do you own this?"

"*Yes.*" I kept my eyes on Ari.

Ari's eyes met mine. "It's nice that you set up the couch for us."

"I didn't. You can sleep in my bed."

"Really?" Sean smiled, clearly misinterpreting that my offer was only for Ari. "How nice, man. I'll put our stuff in there later tonight. Is that your room on the right?"

"It is…" I couldn't believe this shit. The second he walked away to check it out, I glared at Ari. "I need to talk to you *right now.*"

"I don't think so." She shrugged. "I'd be more than happy to talk to you over dinner later today, though. I want to take Sean to Gayle's. I already texted Josh and he's agreed to meet us there at six. You interested?"

"I need to talk to you *alone*."

"If I have time while I'm here…" She sat on the couch and fluffed a pillow. "I'll think about it. Can you hit the light please?"

"*Ari…*"

She stood up and hit the light herself, returning to the couch. "It's nice seeing you again, Carter. You look really good. Happy."

"I'm not happy…"

"Well, *I* am." She gave me a look that said, 'go away' and it took everything inside of me not to turn the light back on and pull her up, to make her listen to what I had to say.

To prevent myself from losing my shit, I went into the guest room and slammed the door shut.

track 29. i wish you would (3:44)

Arizona

I couldn't breathe.

I was pretty sure I was going to pass out in the middle of this awkward dinner if Sean didn't lean over and resuscitate me soon.

Four of us—Josh, Sean, Carter and I were sitting at a table in the back, and with the exception of Carter, we were all getting along. We were going over the menu—pointing all of the best things that he had to try, and Carter was glaring at me. Not saying a word.

I couldn't deny that when I'd first seen him earlier today that my heart had nearly jumped out of my chest in excitement, had almost screamed, "You still love him!" but I'd kept my face stiff and as emotionless as possible.

Even though one touch of his hand had sent my body into a familiar state of overdrive, I was still hurt. Besides, my heart was a fucking idiot.

Sean met all of my spreadsheet specifications perfectly: Smart, witty, subtly stylish, and one hell of a kisser. True, we hadn't had sex and the thought of doing so had yet to even cross my mind, but I was waiting for my heart to lose all hope of Carter before plowing ahead one hundred percent.

Get your shit together, Heart…The man sitting across from me broke you…Remember that…

"So…" Sean looked confused. "This place only serves breakfast food and dessert?"

"Yeah," Josh said. "It's amazing. You can't go wrong with whatever you try."

"I'm not much of a breakfast guy…" He flipped the menu. "Not that big a fan of dessert, either."

"Then why the fuck are you a chef?" Carter muttered under his breath.

Sean didn't hear it, but Josh threw him a pointed look.

"You have to try this," I said, clasping his hand. "Trust me, your life will never be the same."

"Well, when you put it that way…" He leaned over and kissed me. "I'll get this week's specialty waffle plate."

The waitress stepped over at that moment, unknowingly giving us a much needed breather. "Alright, my favorite people… Josh, what are you having?"

"I'm going to try the caramel waffle with peanut butter chips. I'll also have strawberry syrup with it, unless you all have finally taken my suggestion about creating some that's weed flavored?'"

She hit his head with her notepad and laughed. Then she pointed her pen at Sean. "What about you?"

"I'll have the specialty waffle plate."

"What type of syrup?"

"Regular maple will be great."

"Okay, then." She folded her pad and tucked it into her apron. "I'll bring out some more orange juice and some more napkins. Your orders should be ready pretty soon."

"Wait a minute." Sean cleared his throat. "You only took two orders. You didn't get Arizona's or Carter's."

She gave him a blank stare, furrowing her eyebrow. "Good one. I like your sense of humor." She walked away.

"Okay..." He looked at me, confused. "Is only taking half of the orders per table a local quirk I'm not understanding?"

"No, um..." I smiled. "I used to come here a whole lot with—"

"*Me*," Carter said, interrupting. "And since we always order the same thing, there's no need to ask for our order."

Not catching the rudeness in Carter's tone, Sean smiled at me.

"So, Sean..." Josh tried to salvage the night. "Tell me about yourself. Where are you from?"

I tuned him out and sipped my water, meeting Carter's gaze.

I didn't want to admit it, but he looked even sexier now than he did before I left. His jet black hair was cut a little shorter, his lips—even though they were currently pressed together in an angry line, were making butterflies fly around in my chest at the thought of them reconnecting with mine.

I noticed a new tattoo on his forearm, tucked underneath one of his cypress branches, but I didn't dare ask what it was. I wasn't going to ask him anything right now.

Our waitress stepped over to the table again, handing out our orders, and as if she could tell something was wrong with Carter, she didn't bother smiling in his direction. "Let me know if you all need anything. I'll be around..."

"Can you all excuse me for a minute?" Sean stood up, phone in hand. "This is my mother. I forgot to tell her I landed, so I need to take this." He planted a swift kiss on my lips and walked outside.

"So, Josh..." I cut into my waffle. "Are you enjoying—"

"Can you please excuse the two of us for a few seconds, Josh?" Carter glared at me, setting down his knife.

"*Gladly*." Josh immediately walked away, leaving us alone.

"Carter," I said, beating him to it. "Look—"

"You honestly think I don't love you, Ari?"

"What?"

"You heard me." He raised his voice. "Do you honestly think that I don't fucking love you?"

"That's what you said to me before I left, isn't it? Why wouldn't I believe it?"

"Because deep down I know you're smarter than that…" He hissed. "I also know you did not fly all the way here to blow me off and act like you don't know me."

"I came to visit and introduce you to Sean."

"Fuck him." He growled. "Even if I could buy that you liked him—which, you don't by the way, you wouldn't dare introduce him to me so quickly. That's not your style."

"People change."

"We don't," he said. "I still know you like the back of my hand. The only thing that's changed about you since you left is your goddamn hair."

"In your case, your vocabulary has definitely changed," I said, crossing my arms. "You've never cursed at me like this before."

"You've never caught me off guard like this before." He took a deep breath and sighed. "Look, we need to talk whenever you get a chance and have a free hour or two that you can get away from your classmate."

"My boyfriend."

"Yeah, whatever." He stood up and pulled out his wallet. "Find the time and text me when you have a moment. Preferably before this weekend."

"Will you not be sleeping at your house? Won't I see you and be able to tell you a time in person?"

"No," he said flatly. "I got a room at Beach Front Hotel down the street."

"*What?*" I swallowed. "Why?"

"Because first of all, I can't bear the thought of another guy sleeping with you. Second of all, having you in my house and not

being able to touch you…I'm not going to be able to handle that."
He placed a hundred dollar bill on the table. "Call me when you're
ready to talk. Alone."

He left the diner and Sean returned moments later.

Josh didn't, though.

"What happened to your friends?" Sean asked.

"Something important came up so they both had to go."

He shrugged and started to eat his food, and I did my best
to smile and act like the conversation with Carter had never
happened.

track 30. shake it off (3:18)

Carter

Arizona was really testing my patience.

The entire weekend passed without her calling me, and the only thing she texted me was "Thank you for letting me and Sean stay at your place for the weekend. My mom is throwing a 'Welcome Back' dinner for me at her house Tuesday night. She would like you to be there."

I didn't text back. I just drowned myself in legal assignments until my eyes couldn't stay open anymore. It was the only thing that prevented me from showing up to her mom's house and demanding that she listen to me.

"Nonstop seafood, chicken, and waffles made by yours truly, Ari. Be there or else!" Josh announced as he walked into the living room. "Hey, are we going or what?"

"Going where?"

"To Ari's mom's house." He crossed his arms. "You know what I'm talking about. She just sent out a mass text; though, I'm pretty sure she already told you..."

At that second my phone buzzed with the same text Josh had read aloud.

"So, are we going or what?" he asked.

"Not if her so-called boyfriend is there."

"Why are you acting so jealous?" He cut me off.

"Because I am jealous."

"Jesus. Get your shit together, man. You two haven't really talked for over six months. Did you really think no guy would be interested in her over there? That she would just stay single and cry over you until you decided to tell her the truth whenever she got back? Like, I know you only recently realized just how god-damn sexy she is, but…"

"Are you trying to help me or further enrage me?" I gritted my teeth. "For the record, if it's the latter, it's definitely working…"

"Just talk to her."

"I've tried."

"No, you haven't. And you're not trying now. You're growling, pissing everyone off, including the woman you're trying to get back. But honestly, both of you are so stupid, I swear. Maybe you two had the right idea all along, though. Maybe you should've stayed 'just friends.' "

"I'm not trying to hear this from you of all people right now."

"You're not trying to hear anything. That's the problem." He leaned against the wall. "Outside of making dumbass comments all night, what do you plan on doing to get her to listen to you?"

"I'm not sure anymore."

"Bullshit."

"No, I'm honestly not sure. She really has deluded herself into thinking that I only used her for sex last summer, that I didn't love her at all."

"You told her 'not in that way'… That's actually the *worst thing* you could've ever said. What was she supposed to think?"

"That I was doing what was best for her. She's put her dreams on hold for a guy before…I didn't want that."

"You honestly think she would have stayed home from France if you'd told her the truth? Changed her entire future just for you?"

"*Yes.*" I looked up at him, daring him to question is further. "I'm pretty sure I know her ten times better than you do."

He held up his hands in a slight surrender. "Well, if that's the case, what are you going to do now?"

"Try as many times as necessary to make her listen to me..." I stood up. "Let's go."

———

Several months ago...

Before Ari left for France, I'd found her journal in her room. And by "found" I meant she left it open on her desk, underneath her passport and plane tickets.

I wasn't going to read it; I hadn't read it since sixth grade when I teased her about having a crush on the guy she wanted to kiss "so badly that [I] want to see the stars when his lips touch mine." But I saw my name with hearts around it (More than once), so I shut her door while she was downstairs cooking and read:

Dear Janet,

Is it weird that I call you that instead of "journal"? Actually, it's probably weird that I'm twenty three years old and keeping a damn journal to begin with...)

Anyway, I never thought it would happen to me, but I'm in love.

Hopelessly, foolishly, and deeply in love with the last person you'd expect: Carter.

And now I'm not sure what I want anymore...It's true that love puts things in perspective. Before when we weren't having sex, (Yes...we had sex and it was amazing... IN-FUCKING-CREDIBLE actually.) I was hesitant about going away, but now?

Honestly, if he asked me to stay, I would stay. I got into two other culinary programs that are only a few hours away and I can still confirm if need be...I just...My heart has never felt like this before and I don't know what I should do .

Talk to you later,

Ari.

PS—Since I started having Carter over all the time for you know...My room is fucking spotless. You should SEE it! LOL

Knowing Ari like the back of my hand, I knew right then and there that if she did ever tell me that she loved me, it would probably be at the airport right before takeoff. (She was dramatic like that.) That she would probably expect me to say it back, and then she would cry and say that she could learn how to be a better chef in America, that she didn't need to go overseas.

She would stay.

Because she'd done that before for another guy she liked: She went to the University of Pittsburgh—knowing that she didn't really want to go, but she thought she was in love so she followed her heart instead of her dreams.

I loved her enough to want what was best, and I didn't want her to do that again...So, I vowed to be as stoic as possible on the day she left—kissing her one last time definitely, but if she told me she was in love with me before takeoff, I wouldn't let myself say it back.

track 31. you're not sorry (3:22)

Arizona

I stood in the kitchen with my mother, marinating chicken in barbeque sauce while she tossed a salad.

"I like Sean," she said, smiling at me.

"I do, too." I looked outside the window where he was helping Nicole set up seats in the backyard. "He's perfect, honestly."

"How so?"

I thought about pulling out my spreadsheet and showing her how he was a perfect ten in the "intensity of the kisses" and "genuine conversations" categories, but I'd held back.

"He does the sweetest things for me in France—calls me to wake me up every morning, runs with me on the weekends, listens to me whenever I want to talk...He's also an amazing kisser."

She laughed. "An amazing kisser?"

"The best guy I've ever kissed." *Except Carter...*

An image of Carter kissing me at the EPIC party—controlling my lips with his, suddenly ran across my mind and I forced myself to brush it away.

"He said he wants to ask me something over dinner tonight when everyone is here," I said. "You think he's going to propose?"

"This early?" Her eyes widened. "I would hope not."

"He's not." I said, laughing. "I like him a lot, though…You think you could see us together long term?"

"Not sure; although I've always thought you would end up with Carter." She smiled, setting down the salad.

"What? When did you think that?"

"I've always thought that. I still do."

What the… "Do you not see Sean, my current boyfriend, out there?"

"I do," she said. "I think he really cares about you, but I know the two of you aren't in love…I know for a fact that Carter loves you more than you'll ever know."

"Because he's upset that I have a boyfriend? Because he's being rude and mean to me?"

"Because he was here every week that you were gone, asking about you, wanting to know if we'd talked, hoping you would call while he was here."

"Right "

"It's true." She held the cheese grater up to my face and I saw that there were tears welling in my eyes. "I'm not trying to tell you what to do. I'm just telling you what I think, and I think, whether you want to admit it or not, that you belong with Carter."

"He said he didn't feel anything for me when we…"

"When you *what*?"

I sighed. I didn't want to talk about my sex-life with my mom, but she was the closest thing I had to a female BFF so I let it out. "We had sex before I went abroad…We actually had sex a few times…" I paused, waiting for a shocked reaction, at least a gasp, but I got nothing. "And I um…I asked him if he felt something between us changing, because I definitely did. I asked him if he had feelings that were more than friend-like, if he felt like there was something more than sex between us, and he said no."

"You asked him that in person?"

"No. It was in a text message. Same thing."

"It's really not." She clucked her teeth. "Maybe there's a reason he said that."

"Yeah, to tell me the truth and to confirm that we should've never had sex…Could you at least try to look surprised about all of this? I had sex with him. Sex. With. Carter."

She laughed. "I'm not surprised at all, Arizona. I'm only shocked it took this long for it to happen."

"Are you sure you're my mother?"

"I don't think you should make any drastic decisions until you talk to him in person. He's still your best friend." She gave me a light kiss on the cheek and hugged me before walking outside.

I wiped my face on my sleeve and chopped a few more pieces of chicken, cursing myself for not bringing the cutlery set I had in France with me.

Ugh…I'm turning into a cutlery critic…Culinary school symptom number one…

"Arizona?" Sean wrapped his arms around me from behind.

"Yes?" I smiled.

"Can I ask you something?" He kissed the back of my neck and slowly let me go.

"Anything."

"I told you I'll be asking you something in front of everyone at dinner, but before that…" He hesitated. "Would you be willing to leave with me tomorrow?"

"*What?*" That came out of nowhere. "Why?"

"I'm not talking about leaving the States," he said. "Just this part of the beach. You know I only live five hours away so I was thinking we could go see my hometown for a day or two? We can still come back here before flying back to France."

I hesitated, thinking about what my mom said, about wanting to know if Carter had a reason behind hurting me so terribly, but I couldn't think of a single worthy one. "Of course."

He kissed my lips. "Care to join the rest of us outside now?"

"Very much so…" I kissed him back, now hoping that Carter wouldn't show up to see whatever he did have to say…

———

I tried my best to avoid looking at Carter for most of the party, and I could tell that he was avoiding me, too. He'd barely said hello when he arrived; he went straight to my mother, gave her a hug, and sat down at the long picnic table.

Josh, on the other hand, was the one who was surprisingly acting like an adult and talking to Sean and me.

"So, you *have* used marijuana in a recipe before?" Josh leaned forward, looking at Sean.

"I have." He smiled.

"What are the chances of you recreating that little entrée for us while you're in town?"

Nicole slapped the back of Josh's head with a paper plate. "Don't you have exams next week? You shouldn't be thinking about having anything with weed in it. Do your teachers know you smoke?"

"For your information, I don't smoke anymore." He rolled his eyes. "I simply buy products that contain THC and devour them. There's a difference."

We all laughed and shook our heads. (Well, except Carter.)

"Can I address everyone for a second?" Sean tapped his cup with a spoon as he stood up.

Nicole smiled at me, Carter sipped his beer and looked away.

"First," Sean said. "Thank you all for being so welcoming. Ari's told me a lot about you all."

"Clearly not enough..." Carter muttered and Sean shot me a look.

I smiled and shrugged, mouthing, "Ignore him."

He kissed my lips before continuing. "I've lost all of my family in a horrific accident...All of my friends, too..." He winced. "So it means a lot to be around people who remind me that life isn't all terrible..."

Nicole put her hand over her heart.

"Anyway...it's taken years for me to get to a decent place, to feel like living life again," he said, turning to look at me. "And I promised myself that if I found someone who made me feel something again, a feeling that I couldn't ignore, that I would seize the moment because I know, personally, that life is way too short to wait to say something..."

Carter narrowed his eyes at Sean, leaning back in his chair.

Josh took a huge gulp of his drink.

"We haven't known each other that long, Arizona, but..." He clasped my hand. "There's something about you, about us, that makes me feel alive again. I'm not proposing, don't worry—" He laughed. "But I am promising you that if you agree to be mine, I'll be faithful and loyal to you for as long as we're together." He pulled out a small ring, a silver and gold band with an emerald jewel. "This is a promise ring...Do you accept?"

Smiling, I nodded and he placed it onto my finger—kissing my lips as everyone around the table clapped. Minus Josh and Carter.

Josh was shaking his head, murmuring. "This is exactly why I need weed...Even my blood pressure is going up " He stood up from the table and forced a smile. "Congratulations, I'll be right back. I need to get something out of my car."

Sean kissed me again and sat down next to me. "I'm glad you accepted."

"I'm glad I did, too." I smiled back and took his plate. "I'm going to get more dessert from inside. You want anything?"

"Another mini-waffle."

"So, you're a fan of breakfast food now?"

"Only because you made it," he said, still smiling.

I got up and stepped into the house, looking at the ring. It was beautiful, and I immediately knew that between him and Carter, Sean was the safer choice; he wouldn't hurt me.

As I was tossing a paper plate into the trash, I felt familiar hands gripping my waist and spinning me around. Carter.

"Yes?" I asked. "Are you done sulking now? Done growling at me and Sean?"

"I love you." He held me still and looked directly into my eyes. "I fucking love you, Arizona, and I always have…"

My heart immediately raced, but I ignored it. "It's a little too late for that now, isn't it? My boyfriend just made a speech."

"So? You don't love him." He held me tighter. "You just think you like him because he lines up with a few things on your ridiculous spreadsheet."

"Then why did I just accept his promise ring?"

"Because I didn't jump up and stop you." He narrowed his eyes at me. "And you know it."

"You can say whatever you have to say right now. As soon as you let me go, I'm going back to him. A man who actually feels something when we're together—a man who'll actually feel something when we have sex—"

"*If* you ever have sex." He cut me off.

"Did you really just say that?"

"I did and I meant it."

"Let me go. Now."

"No." He bit my bottom lip, preventing me from finishing my sentence. "I've loved you since fourth grade. Since fourth fucking grade."

"Glad you finally have the timeline right."

"Stop it, Ari…" He kissed me. "I just didn't know it. You've been there for every moment of my life and I've been there for yours, too. I do love you, I am in love with you, and I also know you better than you know yourself."

"No, you just *think* you do..."

He ignored my rebuttal. "If I'd told you that I loved you at that airport, you wouldn't have gone to France. You would've stayed here, and I didn't want that for you."

What? My heart stopped, and I hesitated. "What about telling me after takeoff? You still could've told me the truth."

"You had a layover in Los Angeles...You would've come right back."

"No, I wouldn't have."

"Yes. You fucking would have, Ari."

"Then what about—"

"The first week you were gone?" He shook his head. "When you were as miserable in the program as you first were? You would've come home for any reason—especially with me telling you that I loved you...You wouldn't have tried to stay and do your best... You wouldn't have pursued your dream at the best place possible, and you would've settled, possibly regretting it in the long run."

I didn't say anything.

"I regret not telling you sooner, but I sent you letters to try and get this across. Since you were ignoring me, I tried to—"

"Please leave..." I felt tears falling.

"Ari...Please let me finish. There's more I need to say to you."

"No. I've heard enough, and I'm honored you put me before yourself, but...If you really love and respect me, you'll leave... Right now."

He looked as if someone had just sucked the life out of him. But he didn't move.

So, I did.

track 32. you belong with me (3:37)

Arizona

I shut myself in my room and grabbed a pillow off my bed—holding it against my face and screaming into it as loudly as I could.

I did it one more time for good measure, not bothering to wipe away tears. I couldn't believe Carter's reasoning for not saying 'I love you back'. That didn't make any sense. I mean, of course I wanted him to tell me that he loved me back, but for him to assume that I would stay here and cling to him instead of pursing my own dreams? To make it seem like I was that love-struck?

No…I would've left regardless of what he said…I would've—

I suddenly stopped thinking as old memories began to play in front of me, one of the last serious relationships I'd had before Carter and Sean…

His name was Liam and he was supposed to be my soulmate. We were high school sweethearts and we were so cute together that it made Carter sick. Literally. (He got a migraine after being our third wheel at the annual fair, after we kept calling each other "sweetie" and talking about our future together.) Anyway, I'd always believed in planning ahead, and although I wasn't totally convinced, I decided to attend the University of Pittsburgh with him instead of staying closer to home.

Three weeks later, I found out he'd been cheating on me with his ex-girlfriend and I became stuck with a college I never wanted, and a heartache that took over two years to heal.

Still in shock, I grabbed my laptop bag and pulled out the letters he'd sent. (I was originally planning to give them all back to him unopened on the last day of my trip) I thumbed through them all and picked the most recent one, running my fingers along the phrase he'd written on the flap: "URGENT: Please read this, Ari."

Dear Arizona,

I'm not going to bother with pleasantries or waste time telling you about what's going on at home with me because it doesn't matter. Not without you being here anyway.

So, I'll keep this short and to the point.

I didn't mean one fucking word of what I said to you at the airport.

I do love you. I love you 'in that way' and it was much more than sex between us. I only wanted to make sure you left and pursued your dreams instead of staying back for me because I'll always be here for you.

Always.

If I knew that what I said would make you give me the cold shoulder or stop talking to me, I can promise you that I never would've done it and I would take it back in a heartbeat.

Not talking to you for a few days was different.

Not talking to you for a few weeks was torture.

Not talking to you for MONTHS was (and still is) unbearable.

You've always meant the world to me, but it didn't hit me just how much more you meant until you were gone...

I go to sleep, reaching for you—wanting to hear your voice before I shut my eyes. I wake up hoping to have you in my arms, and there are only so many days that I'm going to be able to stay sane without you...

For years we've joked about why I can't last with anyone else for more than six months, and the answer has been right in front of my face all this time: You.

I'm pretty sure it's been you since fourth grade, because now more than ever, I know that I'm supposed to be with you, and you're supposed to be with me.

You belong to me, Ari, and you always will...

You're more than 'just' my best friend, and I never want to be 'just friends' again.

Sincerely (in love with you),

Carter

I cried.

I re-read it a few more times, my heart racing with every word.

I re-folded it and stood up, heading back downstairs to the party. I needed to talk to Sean alone and get the hell away from all my friends and family so I could re-read the letter again before deciding what to do.

Sean's eyes met mine as soon as my feet hit the grass, and he rushed over. "Whoa," he said. "What's wrong with you? Why are you crying? Do we need to go?"

"Yes." I nodded. "Please..."

"Okay." He wiped my tears away, waiting for me to stop. Then he forced a smile and put his arm around my waist.

Out the corner of my eyes, I saw Josh shaking his head at me, saw him seething at me like he was Carter.

I ignored him and gave my mom a hug in the kitchen—avoiding her "What's wrong with you?" expression.

Sean grabbed my bag and we walked into the living room, where a few of my other friends were.

"Leaving already, Ari?" Nicole asked.

"Yeah…I'll be sure to hit you up tomorrow, though." I walked over and gave her a hug. "Thank you everyone for coming. It was good seeing you again."

I gave everyone else hugs, noting that Carter was thankfully long gone.

I got into the rental car with Sean and turned my head toward the window—not saying anything.

"Um…" Sean sounded confused. "Where exactly are we going? All of our stuff is inside…"

"Just drive…"

"Okay…" He placed his hand on my knee and squeezed it, making me feel anything but aroused. I felt guilty and wrong.

He drove around mindlessly for nearly an hour—repeating some of the same streets over and over, and when I was finally able to think straight, I turned to face him.

"Can we stop there?" I pointed at Gayle's.

"Are you hungry?"

"No, I um…" I paused. "I need to talk to you."

"Is it about us?"

"Something like that…" I took a deep breath as he pulled into the parking lot.

He held the door open for me and we walked inside together.

I started to walk toward a booth in the back, but I spotted Carter, Josh, Nicole, and a few other people sitting across the room.

Of course they would think to come here afterwards, too…

I shot them all a short wave, and Carter's deep blue eyes met mine.

Sean pressed his hand against the small of my back and led me over to a table, but I couldn't stop looking at Carter.

"Ari?" Sean asked. "Why does it look like you're going to cry?" He pulled out a handkerchief and handed it to me.

"I'm okay..." I realized Carter wasn't taking his eyes off me, either.

"What do we need to talk about, Ari?" Sean asked.

"Us..." I answered him without looking at his face. "I don't think—"

"You don't think *what*?"

"I don't think I'll be able to keep that promise I made at the party."

"Which part? Why aren't you looking at me?"

"The whole thing, and I'm very sorry..." I noticed Carter standing up and walking over to us. "You're a great guy, and I think you'll make someone very happy one day, but—"

"I'm going to try this one more fucking time." Carter stepped in front of our table, cutting me off. "Arizona Turner, I love you, I am *in love* with you, and I don't give a fuck if you're wearing some other man's promise ring because what you have with him doesn't have shit on what you have with me."

"Excuse me?" Sean looked at Carter, livid. "What the fuck do you think you're doing? Can you not see she's here with me?"

"Not for much longer." Carter kept his eyes on mine. "I sent you a letter every week telling you how I felt, telling you I didn't mean any of what I said at the airport...I've already spent over six months without seeing you, without touching you, and I'm not letting you go back to France without at least *talking* to you— without telling you everything that I have to say."

"Is this shit really happening?" Sean stood up, clenching his fists. "Do you not see me standing here? You think you can just talk to my girlfriend without my permission?"

Everyone in the diner was now silent and staring at the three of us.

"Ari..." Carter stepped even closer to me, reaching down and running his fingers through my hair. "I want you back...I *need* you back..."

"Let's go, Ari." Sean looked at me as he moved around the table. "We need to finish our conversation without this desperate asshole interrupting it."

I didn't get up.

"Ari?" He looked shocked. "Ari, are you seriously considering whatever this asshole is talking about? He's been nothing but rude to you since we got here."

"I've only been rude to *you*," Carter countered, eyes still on mine.

"Ari, if you don't leave with me right now, I'm going straight to the airport and I'm not coming back," Sean said. "I also won't be forgetting this shit anytime soon in France when you go back... What's it going to be?"

I opened my mouth to answer him, but Carter pulled me up and pressed his lips against mine—kissing me as tears fell down my face, as I wrapped my arms around his neck and kissed him back. At that moment, no one else in the diner existed.

It was just me and Carter.

The guy I was in love with, the guy I'd loved for most of my life.

When we finally broke away, I looked over at Sean—to offer an apology, but he was long gone. The other patrons were looking at us with fascination and I blushed as Carter kissed me again.

"I read your letter..." I said softly. "You were right..."

"I usually am."

I narrowed my eyes at him and he smiled, whispering against my mouth. "Let's get out of here..." He pulled me against his side and led me to his car. Taking my hand in his, he looked over at me. "Were you going to go the rest of this trip without saying anything else to me?"

"I was going to come to your house tonight, after I broke up with Sean...You kind of interrupted my break-up speech, though. Pretty sure he'll be smearing my name around all over campus whenever—"

He cut my sentence off with a kiss. "I know it's been a while since we've been together, Ari, but the rules are still the same. I don't want to talk about anyone else when I'm with you, and since I only have four days left before you fly back, I damn sure don't want to waste one second talking about your ex-boyfriend." He kissed me one last time before speeding off into the night.

We made it to his place in record time, and as soon as we were out of the car, his lips latched onto mine and we stumbled up the driveway and into the house with our lips still attached. Knocking over a lamp and a side table, we made it into his bedroom and he immediately pulled me onto his bed.

He took off his shirt and started to unbutton mine, but I grabbed his hand. "Wait, Carter...Wait..."

"What's wrong?"

"Nothing..." I looked into his eyes. "I just...I want to know if..."

"Ask me..." He kissed me, a knowing smile on his lips. "Ask me, Ari "

"No...I guess it really doesn't matter."

"It does." He pulled off my skirt. "Ask me if I've been with anyone else since you've been gone."

"Have you?" I asked, forcing a weak smile.

"No, Ari..." He gave me a reassuring kiss as he unsnapped the front of my bra. "I haven't, and I'd like to keep it that way forever..."

"And what happens when I go back to France?"

"You take the spam filter off my goddamn emails and answer me whenever you get a chance." He unbuckled his pants and let them fall to the floor. "You also invite me up to visit once a month."

"Can you afford to come that often?"

"I can't afford *not* to…" He lay down in the bed and pulled me on top of him. "Are there any other questions?"

"Yes."

He raised his eyebrow, waiting for me to say it.

"What's your new tattoo?" I looked at his arm, and he smiled—holding it up for me to see. "You've always had that Arizona State tattoo…"

"The state, yes…" He pointed to the cursive script underneath it. "Your full name, no…"

I blushed. "I got drunk in France one night when I was crying over you, and I went into a tattoo bar by myself…I must've really been talking shit about you, because the technician misinterpreted what I wanted." I lifted my right arm, showing off the small spot next to my breast where a cursive "Sincerely, Carter" was etched into my skin.

Smiling, Carter traced it with his fingertips. "I love this…Are there any more questions?"

"Yes…I have one more."

"Okay." He gripped my hips, and positioned me over his cock. Then he slowly sucked one of my nipples into his mouth. "I'm listening…"

"In your last letter to me, you said you'd loved me since fourth grade…Not *fifth grade* like you normally try to assert…Do you really think that, timeline-wise, or did you just say that because you knew that would get to me and make me cry?"

"Arizona Turner…" He slowly pulled me down against him— filling me inch by inch, making me moan as he swirled his tongue against my chest. When he was completely inside of me, he held me still and looked into my eyes. "For the record, and the very last time…" He drew my bottom lip into his mouth. "I hated you in fourth grade—absolutely fucking hated you…"

I moaned as he caressed my back with his palms.

"For the first semester anyway..." he whispered. "I did like you a lot more when we became friends. I liked you a lot...But after looking back, yes, I promise that I loved you then..." He slowly let go of my bottom lip. "I love you now." He kissed my lips until I was utterly breathless. "And I always will..."

THE END

acknowledgments

Dear Best Readers Ever,

I want to thank you SO MUCH for reading another one of my books. I can't tell you just how much that means to me, and whether you hated this or loved it, I fucking love you for inviting me to your bookshelf again.

I'm dedicating this entire section to you because without you, I wouldn't have a career, and I promise that I am grateful for that every single day. Every. Single. Day.

I wrote this book because I was in the mood for something different from my norm, so I kept it a secret and didn't tell anyone about it until I was finished. (Jury's still out on whether that was a good idea or not…Though, I must pause here and thank Erik Gevers for a fantastic OMG formatting job and Evelyn Guy for not being upset with me for literally asking her to squeeze me into her editing schedule at the last minute LOL)

Carter & Arizona demanded that their story be told, and they consistently interrupted my other projects with their note-passing and emails, so I had to push them out ASAP.

(This is the part where someone asks, "When is Turbulence coming out?" LOL)

Once again, THANK YOU for taking a chance on Secret Book #1! Is it too early to mention Secret Book #2? (*zipped lips*)

Until next time,
F.L.Y.
(Effin Love You) Always.
Whit

PS—Thank you a million times over to Tamisha Draper, my BFF/"person like they say on Grey's anatomy" for 1)making me finish this book 2) making me release this book and 3) naming this book with the awesome title, Thank you to Bobbi Jo for dropping everything to read this before release and telling me that everything was going to be okay, Thank you to Natasha Gentile for being amazing, Thank you to Alice Tribue for your utter honesty while reading this, and for holding my hand through nervous breakdowns and endless tears, Thank you to the amazing, talented, and inspirational ladies of FYW who I miss terribly (I'll be back after this releases! LOL), Thank you to Brooke Cumberland for your text messages and hilarious bets that get me through rough days, Thank you to Kimberly Brower for being the best agent a girl could ever ask for, and THANK YOU to the countless bloggers and authors who go out of your way to help me. (I'm forever grateful to have such amazing and one-of-a-kind support!!)

Also by Whitney G.

Reasonable Doubt Full Series
Reasonable Doubt #1
Reasonable Doubt # 2
Reasonable Doubt #3

My Last Resolution: A Novella

Mid Life Love Series
Mid Life Love
Mid Life Love: At Last

UPCOMING WORKS
Turbulence (Early 2015)
Twisted Love (Spring 2015)

The Jilted Bride Series (Summer 2015)
Book 1: Scorned
Book 2: Tarnished
Book 3: Burned

Malpractice (Fall 2015)

Printed in Great Britain
by Amazon

39437311R00151